"You have to forgive my mom. She's never tried matchmaking before."

"Is she more subtle than *my* ma~~tch~~ parents?"

"You know your s~~~~ anything more tha~~~~ right?"

"Oh, I know." Chlo~~~~ ~~~~ at him. "Besides, what does your mother expect to happen between us in a few days?"

"I suppose I could ask you to go steady." Zack smiled back. "She's just frustrated that I don't have a girlfriend. Her friends all have adult children who are married with kids. I don't blame her for wanting that for me, too."

"Maybe she just wants to make sure you're well loved."

"I think I've got it," Zack said, chuckling. "Mom's into sightseeing. Let's head to some wedding chapels in Vegas. She could take photos and say she helped us look for the perfect place to get married. What do you think?"

Chloe rolled her eyes and grinned. "This matchmaking thing has warped your brain, Doctor. I think she'd rather go to Disneyland."

Books by Patt Marr

Love Inspired

Angel in Disguise #98
Man of Her Dreams #289
Promise of Forever #350
The Doctor's Bride #429

PATT MARR

graduated from college with honors and with child when she was twenty. She later earned an M.A. in counseling, worked as a high school educator, cooked big meals for friends, attended a zillion basketball games that her husband coached and her son played, and enjoyed many years of church music, children's ministries, drama and television production—often working with her grown-up daughter.

Always a voracious reader, Patt joined Romance Writers of America to learn how to write a book of her own. It took ten years to see her name on a cover, but that book, *Angel in Disguise,* won the National Readers Choice Award for Best Inspirational Romance. She dedicated her second book, *Man of Her Dreams,* to her college sweetheart and lifetime husband, David Marr.

Patt claims to be the happiest woman alive, and why not? She's been blessed with children, grandchildren, wonderful friends and the opportunity to write love stories about people who love God as much as she does.

For more about Patt, please visit her Web site: www.pattmarr.com.

The Doctor's Bride
Patt Marr

Steeple
Hill®

Published by Steeple Hill Books™

STEEPLE HILL BOOKS

Steeple
Hill®

ISBN-13: 978-0-373-87465-1
ISBN-10: 0-373-87465-0

THE DOCTOR'S BRIDE

Copyright © 2008 by Patt Marr

www.SteepleHill.com

Printed in U.S.A.

Now glory be to God who...is able to do far more than we would ever dare to ask or even dream of—infinitely beyond our highest prayers, desires, thoughts, or hopes.

—*Ephesians* 3:20–21

Dedication

To my three "adopted" daughters,

Pam Dokolas, Cathy Ebalo and Teresa Soliz,

and to my daughter, J Marr,

for the laughter and faith that we share.

Acknowledgments

Love and appreciation go to my daughter,
J Marr, for her endless encouragement and
editing skills; to my cousin, Paul Lawrence,
for his faithful critique; to my husband, Dave Marr,
for learning to cook and to Dr. LeRoy Yates for
creating the heroine's medical history.

Chapter One

Beverly Hills, California

Chloe Kilgannon pushed her red clown nose firmly in place and practiced walking in her oversize shoes. When had she last worn them? As a teenager, she'd performed often, but that was a long time ago, and she hadn't clowned since the last time she'd been home.

Home—that was a place not easily defined. If home was where the heart is, it would be wherever there were children who needed the assurance they weren't alone. If she'd still had the job she'd done the last eight years, she could have been heading for a new home today. In India there'd been a horrific mudslide. In Australia, a tornado had touched down. In the aftermath of devastation, there were always newly homeless children separated from their families. Organizing their care and assuring them they were still loved had been her job, a job she'd thought she'd always have.

"Hey, Chloe, are you about ready!"

Nurse Sandy Beechum popped into the hospital's first-floor restroom where Chloe had made her metamorphosis. The two had known each other since Chloe's teenage clowning days.

"Who do you think you are, and what happened to my friend Chloe Kilgannon?" Sandy said, looking her up and down.

Chloe pointed to the painted flower on her cheek and did one of her trademark jiggle-wiggle moves that she'd borrowed from an excited puppy. The ringlets on her purple wig shimmied, and the bells on her collar jingled.

"Well, if it isn't Flower the Clown!" Sandy exclaimed, breaking into laughter. "You funny girl, you haven't changed."

Chloe struck a pose that made her friend laugh, but she was glad that Flower had a painted-on happy face and wasn't expected to talk. If she did, she might break down and tell Sandy how much she *had* changed. Her future would be far different than the one she'd dreamed of.

"All the kids who were able to leave their beds are assembled upstairs in the Sun Room. Is it showtime?"

Chloe made her eyes go wide with anticipation and clapped her gloved hands wildly. She was officially in character, and it was a relief to be somebody else, even for a little while. Flower the Clown could act on any outrageous impulse if it got a laugh.

Dr. Zack Hemingway waited for the elevator, wondering if there was a way to carry a daisy-bedecked basket of sock puppets that wouldn't make people snicker at the sight of him. He'd tried carrying it like a gym bag, but he couldn't get a good grip with springy, fresh flowers decorating the handle. Holding the basket with both hands as if it were a pizza came the most naturally.

The elevator door opened, and Zack did a double take. One of the occupants was a red-nosed clown, who gave him a shy little wave, and the other was Sandy Beechum, a nurse with a whole lot of seniority and even more sass.

"Well, there's something you don't see every day," Sandy said dryly. "Young Dr. Hemingway with a pretty basket. What's in your basket, Doctor?"

"Sock puppets," he said, stepping inside and checking to see if the button for the pediatric floor was lit. It was. He should have guessed that peds was the clown's destination. "I was in the E.R. for a consult when the paramedics brought in a woman who was so frantic about getting this basket to peds that the staff couldn't treat her. Since I was heading there anyway, I volunteered to be the delivery guy."

Sandy chuckled. "I'd have loved to see the staff's reaction to that."

How had Sandy known they'd acted like it was a big deal? Granted, he might not show his softer, more per-sonable side very often—okay, almost never—but his life was all about surgery. He lived it, breathed it, loved it.

"You must be heading for the party," Sandy said. "We have the main attraction with us right now. Flower the Clown, have you met Dr. Zack Hemingway?"

The clown shook her head with an emphatic *no,* and

the bells on her collar jingled. She stuck out her gloved hand for a shake, noticed that he had both hands occupied and shook hands with herself. He had to smile.

"It's nice to meet you, Flower. When I tell my mom I met a real live clown, she's going to wish she'd been here, too. She *loves* clowns! Would you like to meet her?"

Sandy rolled her eyes, and no wonder. He'd sounded as if he were talking to a little kid instead of a clown, though Flower didn't seem to mind. She clapped her gloved hands gleefully, then tucked her hand in his arm. Looking up at him, she nodded as if to say she was ready to go meet his mom.

"Looks like you've got a date, Dr. Hemingway," Sandy said with a chortle.

A really cute date at that. "Flower, I'm sorry, but my mom lives in Illinois."

Flower's head drooped in disappointment.

She was such a good actress that he actually felt bad for her. "But she's coming out here for a visit! It's her birthday!"

Flower perked up in a flash. It was amazing how well she communicated using no words.

"If you give me your phone number, I could set up a meeting." He couldn't believe he was making a date with a clown, but this year he was going all out to make his mother's birthday perfect. One-on-one time with a real clown would make his clown-collecting mom happier than anything he'd planned and he'd made *big* plans.

The elevator door opened onto the peds floor, and Flower stepped out with him, her hand still tucked in the crook of his elbow, clinging to him like a vine. He didn't have the heart to disengage.

"You two look good together, " Sandy said, trailing after them. "And I happen to know that neither of you are seeing anyone."

People were always trying to set him up with their friends, but setting him up with a clown? This was a first. He checked her out, wondering what she looked like under all that makeup. She was fairly tall. He was six foot three, but in her big clown shoes, the top of her puffy purple wig came to his nose.

"What do you think, Flower? Am I your type?"

She looked him over, head to toe, and shrugged as if to say maybe, maybe not. After all that clinging, her indifference made him laugh. A guy had to love a clown who played hard to get.

A nurse on the peds floor saw him carrying the pretty basket and said, "Let me take that basket to the Sun Room, Dr. Hemingway."

She was probably busier than he was at the moment. "That's okay. As you see, I'm escorting Miss Flower to the party, so I'll take the sock puppets and then I'll see my patient Kendra McKnight."

"Kendra's already at the party. You'll want to examine her in her room, but Kendra will be so disappointed if she has to miss the clown."

"How long is your act?" he said to Flower. He didn't want to be the one to disappoint any little girl, and especially not Kendra. Not only had she been a brave child through three surgeries, her mother was a colleague of his.

"Flower never stays long," Sandy answered for the silent clown. "Maybe ten minutes."

He checked his watch. He had time to watch Flower's performance. It would give him something to talk to Mom about. "I'll wait," he said to the nurse.

As they reached the Sun Room, Flower detached herself from him and motioned for him to go on in. Maybe she needed a moment to mentally prepare. He needed that before surgery. He followed Sandy, turned the basket over to a tech and leaned one shoulder against the back wall, his arms folded.

Flower skipped into the room, tripped on her oversize yellow shoes and took a pratfall. It made the kids laugh, especially when she struggled to get up only to fall on her face again. He had to wonder if it truly hurt, though professionals knew how to take a fall.

Moving among the children, she tweaked their noses and invited them to tweak her big red nose. He noticed how gentle she was with the children and how she made them laugh but didn't let them get overexcited. Children who were sick enough to be in the hospital overnight needed to forget how ill they were, and she was superb at her job.

She found a coin behind the ear of a child and showed it to the kids before she "accidentally" swallowed it. Her pretense of choking was so convincing that he geared up to help her, but she staggered among the children, opening her mouth and silently inviting them to find the coin.

One little boy thought she was in trouble though and worriedly called out, "Somebody! Help Flower!"

Flower gave the little a guy a hug before she zoomed

to where Zack leaned against the wall, her arm out-stretched in fake need. Obviously, he was the designated "helper." She turned to the children, pointed to his lab coat with an expression that clearly said, "Is he a doctor?"

Kendra called out, "That's Dr. Hemingway. He's *my* doctor."

He gave Kendra a smile and a little wave.

The clown grabbed his hand and pulled him center stage, the better for all the kids to see. Holding her throat, she looked at him beseechingly.

What was the protocol for the imaginary swallow-ing of a coin? The imaginary Heimlich?

He stepped behind her, circled her with his arms and locked his hands in the proper position. As an ortho-pedic surgeon, he'd never been called upon to do the Heimlich maneuver for real, let alone for pretend, but the kids weren't going to criticize his technique, and the nursing staff was laughing too hard to care.

He didn't apply much pressure at all, but the clown leaned back into him as if he had. Her big yellow clown shoes came at least two feet off the floor. It took three pretend jolts before she coughed into her hand and produced the coin for all to see! He was almost as glad as if he'd helped her for real.

Flower was a bundle of wiggly, over-the-top grati-tude. She shook his right hand and his left hand, but that wasn't enough. She grabbed both of his hands and danced him about as much as he would let her. All of sudden she stopped cold, her hands in the air, her ex-pression one of complete wonder.

The room went silent as they waited for what she would do next. It seemed like a good time for him to inch back to the door, but she snagged his arm. Apparently, he was still part of the act.

She looked at him, her head cocked to one side, and then she slowly covered her heart with both hands. There was no doubting her tender expression. He got it, and so did her audience. Flower was in love. She sighed and made goo-goo eyes at him until every kid and grown-up in the room was laughing.

Zack tried not to. It wasn't nice to laugh at your new girlfriend.

From somewhere she produced a tall stool, apparently for him to sit on. Then she produced an oversize fake diamond ring. She showed it to the kids before getting down on one knee, her intention so obvious that the kids screamed she was doing it wrong. Kendra yelled out, "Flower, you sit on the stool. Dr. Hemingway is supposed to give *you* the ring."

Maybe Flower just wanted to do things her way because she shook her head so hard the curls on her purple wig bounced. He knew she was going to propose even before she reached for his hand. How did a gentleman behave in a situation like this?

"This is so sudden," he said, holding back a laugh. "Can I have a moment to decide?"

She cocked her head and pretended to think about it, then nodded and turned to the kids, swaying left to right, the perfect pantomime of a ticking clock.

When she stopped abruptly and turned expectantly toward him for his answer, he had one. "I'm sorry, but

I just can't think without a sock puppet on my hand."
He turned to the children. "I need a sock puppet. Does
anyone else need a sock puppet?"

Of course they did. The clown clapped her hands as if
she, too, were sock-puppet needy. She jumped to her feet,
and he thought she was going to help with their distribu-
tion, but the next time he looked for her, she was gone.

He found Kendra and asked, "Did you see Flower
leave?"

"No," she said, playing with her sock puppet, "but I
think Flower's special. Sometimes you see her, and then
you don't."

Before she changed out of her clown costume, Chloe
looked at herself in the mirror and tried to imagine what
Dr. Hemingway must have thought about Sandy's
comment that the two of them looked good together.
That was just Sandy teasing, but when Zack had asked
if he was her type, she'd been embarrassed.

If she'd had to answer, it would have been a big *no*.
He'd gone out with both of her sisters! They said he'd
merely been a friend to hang out with, and she believed
them. But anything they did, Chloe made a point of *not*
doing. In any comparison, she came in last. Why set
herself up for that?

But there *was* something about Zack Hemingway.
She'd liked tucking her hand in his arm, and he'd been
great about the pretend Heimlich. And he could be a
Christian. Gentleness and kindness spoke of a Christ-
centered life.

Her older sister, Carmen, stuck her head inside the

door. "So, this is where you are! It took me a while to remember you used to change in this restroom."

"It's still the hospital's least-used restroom." It meant a lot that Carmen had made the effort to find it. As girls, they hadn't been close, but since Chloe had moved into Carmen's house, they'd become best friends.

Chloe turned to the mirror and picked up a hand towel to begin the makeup-removal process, but Carmen touched her arm. "Wait. Let me get a good look at Flower. It's been a long time since I've seen her."

Chloe struck one of the silly poses that came naturally to her as Flower. As herself, she was far more inhibited.

"Adorable," Carmen said softly. "Flower, you are so funny...and so very lovable."

Chloe swallowed hard, working around the lump in her throat. That was a sweet thing for Carmen to say. As usual when she didn't know what to say, she went for the laugh. "Thank you, Carmen. Let me give you a hug."

She took a step forward and Carmen jumped back. "Don't you dare get that makeup on me." Carmen was perfection in her trendy outfit and very high heels.

"Do you ever wear scrubs like a real surgeon?" Chloe teased, toweling off her makeup.

"For surgery, I do. But I like pretty clothes. Tell me about Flower's day. I heard she made a huge hit in the peds unit. I knew she would."

They'd always talked about Flower as a separate person. "It was fun being Flower again."

"I guess so! I heard she proposed to the most eligible bachelor in town."

Chloe had regretted that the moment her knee had

hit the floor. "You know me. I'll do anything to make the kids laugh."

"You made a big impression on Zack. He's been asking around, trying to find out Flower's real identity."

He was? Chloe felt a little zing of joy…which fizzled out too soon. She knew why he was asking. "His mother's coming to town," she said, "and she adores clowns. He probably wanted to set up a meeting."

"Then why didn't he just say, 'Hey! Anybody know how I can get in touch with the clown?' Instead, he's asking exactly the way a man does when he's interested in a woman—as if he doesn't really care if he gets the answer or not."

"Since when did you become an expert on men, Carmen?"

"I'm not, but I know Zack Hemingway. He's interested."

"Did he ask you?"

"Of course."

"And you said?"

"That Flower valued her privacy, and I had to respect that."

"You might as well have told him. Someone will."

"Maybe not. We have new staff who don't know you're Flower. The ones who do know won't risk the chief of surgery's wrath by revealing that Flower is his middle daughter."

"Dad still disapproves of Flower—of me—that much?" She shouldn't be surprised, but it still hurt.

"Dad doesn't approve of anything," Carmen said with a dismissing wave.

"You're his pride and joy," Chloe said without envy. The price Carmen paid for that was too high in Chloe's opinion.

"Would you believe he's still telling people that he fell in love with baby Carmen before he fell for Mom? Dad's still Mom's hero because he rescued her from early widowhood. But enough of that. Tell me. What did you think of Zack?"

"What do I think?" Chloe repeated, giving herself a second to answer. "I think you should have officially dated and fallen for him. He's great."

"He is! And we have everything in common, but I need a partner who'll make me think about something other than surgery."

"Are you sure you gave it enough time?" Chloe switched from her costume to khaki pants and a T-shirt. "Sometimes it takes a while for love to develop."

"I've given it almost two years!" Carmen protested. "I want a man who'll be crazy in love with me, not in *like* with me. Zack's first love will always be surgery."

"You're a surgeon, too. Aren't you the same way?"

"Not quite. I want a husband, a baby *and* my work."

"And Zack doesn't?"

"He's pretty self-sufficient," Carmen said regretfully. "I don't think he needs anyone."

"Except a clown for his mother's birthday party."

"There's that. If he asks, will you say yes?"

"I'll give him the name of a really good clown he can hire. But I never know what Flower will say. She liked the doctor a lot."

Chapter Two

Two weeks later

Chloe could work anywhere in the world and feel at home. The filth and danger that followed catastrophic natural disasters were challenges, but she could sleep on a cement floor, be thankful for any food the Red Cross workers dished up and find the bright side to the worst situations.

So why was she scared out of her mind by her new job? All she had to do was walk into the Beverly Hills Terrace Hotel, follow the signs to her Love Into Action workshop and speak on a topic she knew thoroughly. She had the promise that the Lord would give her nothing too great to bear, not even this new skirt that felt too short and this jacket that felt too snug.

Her sisters had said the suit fit just right, but they'd also said she looked great in it. That had to be more like a confidence builder than a true assessment, but then, what did a T-shirt-and-khaki-pants kind of woman like herself know? Her wardrobe had been perfect for the work she'd done the last eight years. If she had her choice, she would still be doing that job and wearing those clothes, but dwelling on that only made her depressed.

Her grand makeover wasn't much of a morale booster either. She'd liked her natural look, but her sisters had persuaded her to put herself in the hands of pros who'd trimmed her long dark hair and taught her to apply makeup that made her eyes pop and her skin glow. She now owned all these bottles, jars and tubes of makeup that they expected her to use every day.

Since she'd been about six, she'd concluded that God had created her for the express purpose of making her tiny, beautiful sisters look adorable in comparison to herself, but that wasn't *quite* as true since her makeover. The ugly duckling had become something of a swan. Sort of an apprentice swan. A tall apprentice swan.

She still towered over her sisters, but she'd gone shopping with them last week without dreading it as much as usual. That hadn't lasted long. They'd looked appalled at everything she'd pulled off the rack. Granted, she was eight years behind in fashion trends, but was her taste that bad?

At least her suit today was blue, her favorite color, and she loved her new strappy heels. She still wobbled when she walked in them, but they added inches to her height of five feet nine and made her feel really, really tall. From this view she could look anyone in the eye. And she couldn't miss the sign atop a conference-room door that read The Clayton Room.

That was supposed to be her room, but there had to be some mistake. This room was way too big. This was not the small, intimate environment she'd been promised for her first speaking engagement. Even when she'd pictured herself in a small room with a handful of people, she'd felt queasy. But this room! Her knees sort of buckled, and she sank to a chair on one of the aisles.

Aisles! More than one!

Lord, help! You know my heart. I want to serve You, but I can't do this! Maybe this new job isn't Your will, or maybe I'm just in the wrong room.

"Chloe! I see you've found your room." A personable, gray-haired man extended a welcoming hand. "I'm Craig Zook, the workshop coordinator."

"It's nice to see you, Craig." Her voice came out steady, despite her near-panic. "I think I must be in the wrong room."

"No, this is all for you," he said with a satisfied smile, scanning the many chairs. "I know it's not what we discussed, but blame the room change on these pictures in the program. You're in every one with children from Bangladesh, Thailand, Indonesia, Nicaragua, Peru and places I've never heard of."

"Since I don't have experience as a speaker, my supervisor thought the pictures would give me credibility."

"Then, mission accomplished! You've created quite a buzz, Chloe Kilgannon. Our conferees want to see the speaker who's lived her topic, 'Loving Children—Face to Face.' I know God's going to use you today."

She'd come here, believing that.

Conferees were drifting in, so she headed for a chair near the stage. Maybe she could pray her panic away. She opened her program to the pictures and felt the familiar heart tug of loving these children.

When she'd first been told that her bout with dengue fever meant the end of fieldwork, she'd thought her heart would break. How could the Lord use her better as a seminar speaker? Raising public consciousness to the need of loving children more was a job that needed doing. And she would do it…if she could make it to the stage without throwing up.

Dr. Zack Hemingway waited at yet another red traffic light, the seventh since he'd been counting. He could see the Terrace Hotel from here, and he could imagine his mom sitting alone at the Love into Action conference, wondering if he would show up for the last workshop before lunch or if he'd show up at all. He'd said he would meet her for breakfast, but an emergency surgery had changed that.

The day after his dad's funeral three months ago, when she'd mentioned how much she wanted to attend the Love into Action conference here in L.A., he'd wanted to shout. Not only was Mom making plans for a new life, he could give her a gift that didn't involve him "settling down," which was Mom-talk for saying she wanted grandkids.

The light changed and Zack inched forward in the heavy traffic. Another five minutes and he'd be sitting in the workshop she'd chosen. It had to do with the global needs of children. They'd show those heartbreaking pictures of little kids with their tearful eyes and ask for donations. He would rather write a check, skip the conference and drive Mom up to Santa Barbara for a day of fun in the sun.

Finally, Zack pulled into the Terrace Hotel drive, tossed his car keys to a parking valet and took off at a jog. What was the workshop called? Loving Children— Face to Face?

He hurried toward the right room, straightening his tan suit jacket. Mom said the color looked best with his hair, a nondescript brown cut so short it couldn't possibly matter. He tightened his blue tie, a present from her because it matched his eyes. Would she notice he'd made the effort?

Finding the Clayton Room was easier than spotting Mom. The room was packed, and every chair seemed to be taken. There she was—second row, center— sitting beside an empty chair. She must have had faith he would get here.

He slid in beside her and said, "Sorry, I'm late."

"But you're not," she said, giving him one of her sweet smiles, complete with dimples. "It's just starting."

From her seat near the stage, Chloe stopped praying long enough to glance around. It looked as if every chair was filled. Bile rose in her stomach.

"Hi Chloe, I'm Marilyn James, your workshop moderator."

The lovely woman extending her hand looked familiar. Most of the moderators were Hollywood celebrities, but Chloe was too out of touch to recognize her.

"Are you ready?" the woman asked with an encouraging smile.

Chloe opened her mouth to say she was fine. When absolutely nothing came out, the moderator gave her an understanding look and took one of her hands.

"It's only a little stage fright. Let's pray about it, Chloe."

Chloe closed her eyes and gripped the woman's hand.

"Father God, You've given Chloe experiences that we need to hear about today. Strengthen her in every way. Help her remember that she speaks for You, and give her the assurance that You will have the right words for her to say when she needs them. In Your Son's name, amen."

"Amen," Chloe echoed, feeling more like herself. How could she have let herself get so worked up when this was all about the Lord and His children?

"I'm going to introduce you now. Okay?"

"Perfect. Thank you, Marilyn."

She headed for the dais, and Chloe told herself that all she had to do was stay calm until she made her opening remarks. Then the house lights would dim and she would be in the dark, talking about her friends on the big screen. The children were the story.

"Good morning," Marilyn began, speaking into the mike. "Our speaker grew up right here in Beverly Hills. At the age of twenty, she'd graduated magna cum laude from UCLA and completed her course work for her Ph.D. Her travels began as research opportunities, but turned into long-term humanitarian service.

"From news reports, you've heard of devastating

natural disasters all over the globe, but our speaker has been there, on the scene, setting up the care of children separated from their parents."

The longer the woman spoke, the less calm Chloe felt. Her heart raced, her breath came in short, rapid spurts and she couldn't think of anything she'd planned to say.

"This workshop will present information on short-term international service and give suggestions for long-term ways to show love close to home. Ladies and gentlemen, please welcome home our speaker…Chloe Kilgannon."

The audience applauded and Chloe stood. If she put one foot in front of the other, she could make it. Had anyone ever died of stage fright? Would she throw up first or just pass out? Would there be a doctor in the house?

Zack watched the speaker approach the podium and wondered if there could be *two* Chloe Kilgannons. Carmen and Cate said he'd met their sister, but he couldn't have forgotten this attractive, poised woman. She stood at the podium, looked across her audience and smiled. Wow! What a great smile.

"She's lovely, isn't she?" his mother whispered.

It was on the tip of his tongue to say she was terrific, but if he didn't check that impulse, no doubt Mom would find a way to introduce him to Chloe. He'd rather handle it on his own.

Chloe held on to the podium with both hands just in case her knees gave way. She was that nervous. Nearly every seat was taken, which was amazing considering she was a nobody. They hadn't shown up to hear a famous speaker, so that had to mean they wanted to make a difference for the Lord. That soothed her nerves and gave her the boldness to begin.

"When God puts a passion in your heart for His children," she said, the words coming out with surprising ease, "your life is enriched beyond measure. The last eight years of my life have been all I could have asked for, even though the living conditions were far from the luxury you and I take for granted. I've come to define *luxury* as warm water to bathe in and cool water to drink, clean air, a change of clothing, a blanket, an umbrella, a toothbrush, a picture of a loved one.

"I've discovered that luxury such as we know becomes a cocoon—a comfortable place that prevents us from experiencing the exhilarating joy of helping people who really need us—children who need us, children like these."

Chloe nodded to the projectionist. The house lights dimmed and the first picture of her little friends appeared on the screen. Just as she had hoped, standing here in the dark, looking at children she loved, her nerves vanished and she wasn't scared anymore.

Zack's eyes adjusted to the dark, and pictures of children flashed across the screen behind Chloe. In the ambient light from the projection, her slenderness gave her a youthful appearance but she had to be in her late twenties.

"You'll notice that most of these children are well

dressed and well nourished. Their physical needs have been attended to."

None of the photos stayed on the screen more than a few seconds, but the quantity of them made a big impact.

"Many of these children lost their homes, their family members and all that was familiar, but mixed in with their pictures are those of children who live right here in the U.S.A. They live in your neighborhoods. They may lack for nothing materially. They might even *have* family, yet they share a common denominator. Do you see it?"

The pictures went on and on. As a doctor, Zack had seen misery on many levels and had assumed he was beyond shock, but he'd been wrong. Looking at these children caught him off guard. From the silence in the room, he wasn't the only one.

Kids who knew they were being photographed usually rose for the occasion and showed plenty of personality, no matter how sick or miserable they were, but not these kids.

"They look lost, don't they?" Chloe said softly, as if she hated to speak at all. "You may have already guessed that the common denominator is the lack of love in their lives. No government can guarantee love for its youngest citizens, yet, without it, there's no joy, no hope for a better tomorrow."

He could see what she meant, and it got under his skin.

"The children in your life need your love," the speaker said simply. "And the good news is that you are here. That must mean you care."

She was giving him more credit than he deserved.

He hadn't thought about any of this before, but he should have.

"Most people feel like a monetary gift is all they can provide, and it is a significant expression of your love, but dollars alone won't put hope back in the eyes of children. When you want to reach out in a personal way and need to know how, Love Into Action can point you to reputable agencies who never have enough volunteers. Would you pray with me about what we can do together?"

Zack reached for his mom's hand, just as she'd taught him to do when was he was little.

"Father God," Chloe prayed, "we ask that You show us how we are to love Your children. We want to be Your voice, Your hands, Your feet. Lord, use us…in small ways or big…in our own communities or in faraway places. Through us, Lord, let children feel love, joy and great blessing."

Zack's emotions seesawed from wanting to do all he could do to wishing his mother had asked for a birthday cruise. If he were being asked for money alone, he could write that fat check and let his conscience move on.

Chloe then talked about their workshop packets and invited conferees to call, write or e-mail her. There was no hard sell on her part and no overly impassioned plea for their participation, only the statement that she was there to help if they needed it.

"Let me end with this thought," she said, looking at the final screen, a picture of a little girl holding her older brother's hand, both of them so pitifully sad that Zack felt a sting of tears behind his eyes. "When you think of the overwhelming need…when you know it's more than you can possibly handle…you will be right."

She'd read his mind. He didn't want to fail kids like these, but what could he do, outside of writing that check?

"You can do more than you think you can." She paused as if she searched for the right words to bring her message home. "Remember that *something* is better than *nothing*. The one smile, the one look of recognition, the one kind word you give to a child may be the *only* one he receives today."

Zack hated to believe that was true, but if it hadn't been for his mom's smiles and encouragement, he could have been just as sad as the kids on the screen. Would he have had the courage to achieve what he had?

His mom wiped tears from her cheeks.

Chloe was good. Really good. She had him wondering how he interacted with kids in his life. Did he ignore them while he talked to their parents? Did he ever kneel to meet their eyes?

And she had him wondering about her as more than a conference speaker. How could a guy help but admire a woman like her? Was she single? With all that world travel, she might be.

How was he going to meet her? He was terrible at making the first move. If his mother so much as sniffed at his interest, she'd make it for him, he'd be embarrassed, and his chance to know this cool woman would be over. It might be awkward, but he had to make that first move.

Chapter Three

The house lights came up, and Chloe invited them to look through their packets. "There are plenty of ideas on how you can love the children in your own community. If you want the experience of serving in other countries, there's information about short mission options and extended opportunities."

She continued, raising her voice to accommodate the rustling sound of conferees looking through their packets. Zack watched his mother dig through hers. If she wanted to love children at one of those foreign locations Chloe had mentioned, he would gladly pay her way.

His best friend, Collin Brennan, an anesthesiologist, had mentioned a medical missionary trip. Collin's wife was a nurse, and Zack could provide the surgical skills. Zack hadn't paid much attention before, but it certainly was a possibility. Collin could put the kids to sleep while Zack used his scalpel to help them, but didn't it make more sense to fly them to the U.S. where they could get first-class care?

Toward the end of question-and-answer period, his mother raised her hand. Chloe nodded, giving his mom the floor.

"Ms. Kilgannon, thank you for…"

Chloe looked at his mother, saw him and did a visible double take. She knew him. There was no doubt about that.

Was that good…or really, really bad? He nodded, which seemed like the right thing to do even if he didn't have a clue when or where they'd met.

With a shadow of a smile, she nodded back and focused again on his mom. "Excuse me, could you repeat the question? I'm afraid I wasn't paying attention because I just noticed the very nice man you're sitting next to."

Mom looked at him with shock. "Zack? You know Chloe Kilgannon?"

"A couple of weeks ago," Chloe said, "a friend had asked me to do my act as Flower the Clown at the hospital.

"This man is a doctor who was on the pediatrics floor to check on a patient. Since he seemed like a very kind man with an excellent sense of humor, Flower—*not me*—took advantage of his goodwill and drew him into the act."

The crowd responded with "ooh's" of understanding.

Chloe looked down at Zack and saw that he'd put it together. His smile, so big and wide, made her wobble in her new high heels. "I'm telling you this because what he did that day is a perfect example of loving children, face to face. Just by playing along and helping the children forget how sick they were, he made a difference."

She glanced back at Zack and was surprised that he looked at her with amazement. Hadn't he realized that he'd done a good thing?

"Did he want to be the subject of Flower's silliness? Probably not! But he left his comfort zone to do something good for the kids. Wasn't that great?"

All over the room people nodded and some applauded.

"I hope you'll let me know when you've experienced new ways of showing children they are loved. You'll feel so good about it, and so will I. Thank you for being a great audience."

As Chloe stepped away from the podium, the audience rose to their feet and applauded. The workshop moderator hugged Chloe, and that was it. Her first presentation was over.

People gathered around her for more questions, and she lost sight of Zack. Her disappointment was as keen as a child who'd watched her pretty balloon float away, but she had to focus on the people who wanted to talk to her.

Finally the moderator interceded and sent everyone to lunch. The crowd thinned, and *there* was Zack, his arms crossed and that great smile on his face. He came toward her with an outstretched hand. "Hi, Chloe. It's nice to meet you as yourself."

Though she'd just shaken dozens of hands, the touch of his hand sent a little shiver of excitement up her spine. "I should confess, when we met in the hospital elevator, I *did* know who you were. My sisters had pointed you out at Collin Brennan's wedding."

"You were there? I sat with your family, but—"

"I was at the children's table, keeping them entertained as Flower."

"You're very good at that," he said with awe. "Now

that I know *how* good, I probably shouldn't get my hopes up that Flower genuinely fell for me, should I?"

"Flower hoped you'd forget that."

"Forget? I never forget a red-nosed woman who literally falls at my feet."

"You know, I hurt my knee on that move."

"I'm sorry," he said, switching from a smile to a look of genuine concern. "Knees are my orthopedic sub-specialty. Does it still bother you?"

"No, but I'll never do that particular fall again."

"Good!" His grin was back. "Flower shouldn't fall for just any guy."

She knew he was teasing, but she felt a little zing of joy. "I never know what Flower will do next," she said, trying to explain away her silliness.

"When she works the peds floor again, have her give me a call. I'll be her straight man any day. It isn't much, but I have it on good authority that anything we do for kids is better than nothing at all."

Chloe felt a smile deep in her soul. "Thanks for remembering that."

"I think everyone did. You could have heard a pin drop. You're a very good speaker, Chloe."

The sincerity in his sky-blue eyes had to be real. "Thank you. This was my first presentation, and I thought I would be sick."

"When you walked on stage, you seemed a little nervous. I even asked the Lord to help you. But then you seemed so poised I thought I must have been wrong."

"You didn't consider that your prayer could have helped?" she teased.

"Not even once," he admitted with a rueful smile.

"Well, it may have, along with the prayers of my coworkers. They all knew I felt as if I were going to the gallows."

He shook his head and grinned. "Seriously, you were terrific up there. My mother thought so, too."

"That was your mother beside you?"

He nodded. "This really made her day, her birthday, as a matter of fact."

"*That's* why you're here!" Chloe said, putting it together. "I did wonder."

"You don't see me as guy who's interested in loving children, face-to-face?" he quipped.

"*Everyone* can love children, face-to-face," she said, teasing back. "But I know how busy surgeons are. I can't see my dad or my sister taking time to attend a conference like this."

"You're right," he said candidly. "I'm here for Mom. My dad died recently, and Mom's looking for a new direction for her life. I think she's found it."

"I hope so! I want to meet her, but I'm due in the conference dining room. Each speaker hosts a table. Perhaps you and your mother could sit with me."

"Mom would love that! I'm supposed to meet her outside the ladies' room. Shall we surprise her?"

Walking out of this big room with Zack Hemingway she felt so different than she'd felt walking in. She'd been scared to death, but look at her now! She had the attention of the most sought-after bachelor in Beverly Hills.

He was quite a bit taller that she was, six feet two

at least. She always noticed a man's height because she was taller than average. Zack's clean-shaven jaw angled before squaring off a bit at the chin, and his nose was less than perfect, which she liked a lot, considering the man lived in the plastic-surgery capital of the world.

His tan suit looked as expensive as the ones her father wore and probably was, the way it fit his wide shoulders so well. Usually she preferred the rugged look of a guy in a T-shirt and jeans, but Zack in a suit and tie looked…

Though she had an IQ of 170 and a vocabulary to match, *yummy* was the word that came to mind.

Zack put his hand on Chloe's elbow and stopped their progress outside the restroom. "This is where I agreed to meet Mom," he said.

The words were barely out of his mouth when a pretty blond woman in a pink suit and low-heeled pink pumps entered the hallway. She spotted Zack right away, but when she saw Chloe, her blue eyes lit up as if it were Christmas.

"Oh, Chloe! Zack said he would introduce us, and here you are!" She embraced Chloe in a light hug.

"Chloe, this is my mother, Bonnie Hemingway, a retired high school biology teacher from East Moline, Illinois—my hometown."

"I'm happy to meet you, Mrs. Hemingway," Chloe said, impressed with the joy of life this woman seemed to have.

"Please, call me Bonnie. Chloe, your presentation touched my heart more than I can say."

"I'm so glad. I've never been more nervous in my life."

"It didn't get the best of you! You're a natural-born speaker and teacher."

"Thank you," Chloe said from the bottom of her heart. "You don't know how I appreciate the encouragement."

"I couldn't believe it when Zack said he knew your family."

"And even when the moderator said your name, I couldn't believe you were Sterling's daughter," Zack added.

"You didn't recognize me?" Chloe asked with feigned dismay. "After all we've meant to each other?"

"I know! What can I say?" He hung his head in mock shame.

"Oh, I wish I'd been there to see your clown act!" Bonnie said. "I love clowns! I even collect them."

"She does," Zack affirmed with his great smile. "She has all kinds. Salt and pepper shakers, figurines, you name it. Is there any possibility that Flower could make a special appearance in honor of Mom's birthday?"

For the opportunity to spend time with this guy, it was a done deal. "Flower *loves* birthday parties, but she's pretty busy today."

"I'm here until a week from Monday," Bonnie said.

"Name the day, Chloe. This is Mom's week. Not only is it her birthday, it's her first visit to California. I took vacation time, so I'm available as a chauffeur, sock-puppet carrier or anything that doesn't involve *me* in a clown suit."

"Bonnie, would you like a clown lesson from Flower?" Chloe asked.

"Oh, my! Yes!"

"You'll have to decide on your clown name and persona so we can design your makeup and costume."

"I'll have my own clown personality?" Bonnie's blue eyes sparkled at the thought.

"Well, sure. Once you're in costume, you're not you anymore."

"This will give me something to think about! Chloe, this has been such a pleasure. I wonder if you could join Zack and me for lunch? It would be so special to celebrate my birthday with you."

"As a speaker, I'm hosting a table. I thought you and Zack might join me."

"But of course we could. That would be marvelous!"

"I should be there now."

"Then we shouldn't dawdle. Those tables could be filling up fast." Bonnie turned to walk ahead.

Zack fell into step beside Chloe. "That's my mom, leading the way."

"She's wonderful," Chloe said softly before turning to catch up. She would love to have a close relationship like that with her own mother.

"Mom, I need to call the hospital. You two go ahead and grab those seats. Okay?"

Bonnie waved him on, then took Chloe's arm and set a pace that would get them there quickly.

"Chloe, are you seeing anyone?" she asked bluntly.

"No," Chloe answered, wondering where this was going.

"I hope you'll forgive a mother for saying so, but I think you and Zack would make a perfect couple."

Bonnie had said she collected clowns, but this took

hobbying to a whole new level. "Your son, the doctor, and Flower the Clown?" Chloe teased.

"No, my son, the man who says he's too busy to fall in love and have a family, and Chloe, my tender-hearted new friend who seems to know that a life without love is no life at all."

Chapter Four

Zack draped his arm over the back of his mother's chair, the better to observe Chloe during the luncheon speaker's presentation. In this environment she was a star, though no one would think it from her humble attitude. Humility wasn't a Kilgannon trait he'd noticed before, but it seemed to be as much a part of Chloe's personality as her sense of humor.

It took very little to make her laugh. A minute ago the speaker had made a comment that Zack thought was funny even if the others at the table didn't. Chloe had glanced at him, seen that he had no reservations about holding back a grin and burst into a goofy little giggle. It had only lasted a second, but for him it was the high point of the luncheon.

What a shame that he hadn't followed his instincts after he'd met her as Flower two weeks ago. He remembered thinking how good the clown was at her job—which, as it turned out, wasn't her job at all, but something she did to show love. When she'd disappeared, he'd made a halfhearted effort to find out her real name, but he'd told himself it was so Mom could meet the clown.

The clown—that was how he'd thought of her that day, not even as Flower. Had he become so self-absorbed that individuals weren't important to him unless they had something wrong with them that he could make better? And if he had, could he change? Did he even want to?

He liked his single life just as it was, and he'd worked very hard to get what he had. His Mercedes, the expensive clothes and his condo—they were all nice, but not what he'd aimed for. What he really wanted was the opportunity to give people a pain-free life. Lots of people, lots of surgeries, lots of time in the OR—his favorite place to be.

Chloe turned her head toward him, but slowly as if she were studying the entire audience. He waited for her gaze to land on him, which it did for a nanosecond before it skittered past. Was she interested in him?

He hadn't been nearly as subtle when he'd checked her out. He'd stared long enough to notice that her long dark eyelashes curled at the ends, that her eyebrows arched over her remarkable eyes and her nose tipped just at the end. Chloe was pretty, really pretty, and really sweet. Around her a man could lose his heart if he wasn't careful.

She hadn't looked his way again, though the luncheon speaker was long-winded and not half as interesting as Chloe had been in her workshop. Was Mom enjoying the speaker?

He glanced at Mom, and his heart sank. She was

having the time of her life…and probably hadn't heard one word of the speaker. Her eyes flicked from Chloe to him as if she were watching a tennis match.

He leaned over and whispered, "What are you doing?"

"Never mind," she whispered back. "I know what's going on. I'm going to invite Chloe to my birthday dinner tonight."

"Good." Sometimes he ran out of things to talk about with his mother. It would feel like more of a party with Chloe along.

All this matchmaking was giving him a headache. He rubbed the back of his neck and told himself everything would be back to normal a week from Monday. Mom would be back in Illinois and he'd be back in the OR, where he didn't have to deal with people and how they felt until their anesthesia wore off and he could prescribe something for real, physical pain.

Dealing with people and their feelings was tough. He would love nothing more than to give his mom a hug and say, "I know you want grandchildren, but, please, can't it be enough that I'm happy?"

Because his mom loved him, she would nod and try to hide how it crushed her, and he would feel terrible. He never wanted to disappoint her…if he could help it.

Chloe hadn't heard much of the speaker's presentation. She'd been too busy thinking that she'd finally met someone with boyfriend potential, but Zack was her polar opposite. She wanted to raise children who would know what it meant to be loved, and Zack had a reputation for not needing anyone.

Her sisters, Carmen and Cate, agreed that he was a great guy. He didn't have an inflated ego, which was a remarkable quality considering the attention he got from the doctor-groupies who seemed intent on becoming the second half of "Dr. and Mrs."

Chloe had never understood women like that. Didn't they realize that they would see their pool guys more than they would see their husbands? At least that was the way it had been in her house. Surgeons like her dad lived at the hospital.

When the speaker finally finished, Chloe gave Zack's mother her business card. "Call me when you know when you'd like that clown lesson, Bonnie. I'll be out of town next weekend doing a workshop, but any weekday after four is fine."

"That's so nice of you, Chloe."

"Well, it *is* your birthday."

"Oh! You have to see what Zack did for my birthday. Could you come up to my room for a minute? I've got to share this with someone."

"I'd love to!" How could she turn Bonnie down?

"I see someone I'd like to talk to," Zack said. "You two go ahead, and I'll meet you upstairs."

When Bonnie opened the door to her room, Chloe could see why Bonnie had been so impressed. The place had *California luxury* written all over it. Outside the balcony, the tops of tall palm trees swayed in the breeze. On the bar counter was a basket of luscious-looking fruit, and centered on the dining table was an enormous bouquet of roses.

"Bonnie! What a wonderful place to celebrate your birthday!"

"I'm staying with Zack for the rest of my visit, but he wanted me to have a room at the hotel during the conference. A room, Chloe! Do you call this a room?"

"I call it the effort of a son who wants to show his mother he loves her."

"But he's done so much. He set up a day at a spa back home for me to have a makeover. He made sure I had new clothes, and he flew me out here first class. I feel like Cinderella!"

Chloe laughed at the woman's exuberance. "I'm sure you deserve it!"

"On top of everything else, he had the roses waiting for me—sixty of them—one for each year I've lived. I didn't know I'd raised such a thoughtful son...or that he could afford all this!"

"From what I hear, Zack has become *the* orthopedic surgeon to see in Los Angeles. His patients are among the most celebrated in a town full of celebrities."

"Really?" Bonnie's blue eyes rounded with pleased surprise. "I wish Zack's dad could have heard that. Zack had so many achievements, but Roland never had a kind word for Zack. It made me so mad."

Chloe had to wonder why Bonnie had put up with that. She was a teacher. She knew how withholding praise affected a child.

"Zack seems happy, but I have to wonder if he isn't lonely."

"Being alone isn't the same thing as being lonely. Maybe he's just wrapped up in his work. That's how it's been for me."

"Chloe, you're such a wonderful person. I can't believe you haven't found your Mr. Right by now?"

Bonnie's woeful expression struck Chloe as funny. "It's okay, Bonnie. I haven't really been looking for him."

"And now that your life has changed directions?"

"I don't know if I'll find Mr. Right. Many women don't. Outside of literature, do you think people experience that earth-shattering love that we read about?"

"Yes, I do. I felt it for Zack's father. Sometimes it doesn't seem to last, but it's what I want for my son and all my single friends."

It was hard to believe this lovely woman claimed that kind of love for a man who hadn't taken pride in his son. It wasn't for Chloe to judge, but how could Bonnie have loved that man?

There was a knock on the outer door before Zack entered, holding up the card key he'd used to get in. "Am I interrupting?"

"You are, but in the best way," Bonnie said. "Chloe and I have been talking like old friends. I haven't even gotten around to asking her if she'll join us for dinner tonight. Can you celebrate with me, Chloe?"

The invitation came as a surprise, but who could say no to this nice woman? "I'd love to join you, Bonnie."

"Great!" Zack said. "Chloe's sister is joining us, too."

"How wonderful. It *will* be a party!" Bonnie exclaimed. Bonnie must have told Zack she was inviting Chloe for dinner, and Zack must have called at least one of her sisters. "Which sister, Zack?"

"Carmen. I called Cate, too, but she had plans."

Bonnie's eyes narrowed. "Zack, if you can invite these women at the last moment, you must know Chloe's sisters very well."

Zack sent a silent SOS to Chloe. As intelligent as she was, she had to have realized that Mom was in match-maker mode. With more people around, Mom couldn't zero in on just the two of them.

Chloe's eyes said she got it. "Bonnie, Zack is a favorite in our community, professionally and socially."

That was good so far. He threw her a grateful glance.

"In fact," Chloe continued, "he's such a favorite that my parents are hoping Zack will choose a Kilgannon bride. Our mother is rooting for my younger sister, Cate, but our dad is staunchly behind Carmen, my older sister. She's the one you'll meet tonight."

"Oh my!" his mother gasped.

Zack almost groaned out loud. Chloe hadn't lied, and everyone in the Beverly Hills medical community knew it, but did his mother have to know?

"I don't believe you've mentioned this before, Zack," his mother said in her teacher voice. "Is Carmen the sister you're interested in?"

"Chloe's sisters are my friends, Mom. Just that. Friends."

"Then why do their parents expect you to marry one of them?"

He felt sweat break out on his forehead. "Possibly for the same reason you're hoping I'll find someone."

A smile broke through the tension on her face. "Then, good for them!"

"Bonnie, my parents are fierce matchmakers," Chloe said.

He held his breath, hoping she wouldn't make it worse.

"Mom and Dad began their courtship of Zack two years ago. It was the first night I ever saw him, but we didn't meet."

"And why not?" his mother asked before he could.

"Zack and I talked about that before lunch. We were at a wedding reception. He sat with my family, but Flower the Clown entertained the children at the kids' table."

"And you wore pink!" he said, suddenly remembering. "Pink hair, pink costume, pink clown shoes—"

"It *was* the bride's color," Chloe said with a grin.

"I remember! You were so cute."

"Thank you! Bonnie, Zack can be excused for his lapse in memory. The poor guy was on sensory overload sitting between my sisters and across from my mother. They're charming and far more than *cute.*"

They were gorgeous, but he remembered how adorable Flower had been and how she'd been completely undeserving of her father's harsh admonition to "grow up." He particularly remembered Sterling saying that, and his respect for the man had taken a nosedive.

"I remember trying to talk to you that night," he said.

"Flower doesn't talk," she replied with a grin.

"That's why I said 'trying.' I wanted to get to know you."

"You did?" She seemed surprised...and pleased.

"Sure, I even called you at your parents' house, but you were gone."

She thought for a moment. "That was the mudslide in the Himalayas. It took out a whole village."

"How terrible," his mother said. "Chloe, you've lived a remarkable life for such a young woman. I'm eager to hear more about it at dinner tonight, and I'm looking forward to meeting your sisters, who are such good friends of my son."

"Just Carmen tonight, Mom," he corrected.

She gave him a knowing glance. "Carmen tonight, but *Cate* very soon."

Okay, Mom had made a point of showing him she remembered both names and forgot nothing. His plan had been to steer clear of the Kilgannons while Mom was here to avoid all this, but Chloe had stirred the pot and left him in hot water. And what did she think of herself?

A glance said she was enjoying herself way too much.

Chloe picked up her purse and her gift for Bonnie and met Carmen standing by the front door, tapping her foot. "I'm *not* late," Chloe said defensively.

"I know, but if I'm not early, I feel late," Carmen replied, leading the way to her car. "Why are you carrying your shoes? I'm pretty sure it's 'no shoes, no service' at The Hilltop."

"I'll wear them, just not until I've gotten past these broken tiles that pass as a path. I'm not as good at wearing these stilts as you are."

At the car, Chloe slipped her new shoes on. They were only a couple of straps across her toes, but they did make her legs look great. Sliding into the passenger side of Carmen's sports car, she reached for her seat belt. It would wrinkle her new dress, but a few wrinkles might make her feel more like herself.

With her long hair swept up at one side and secured by one of Cate's combs, she hadn't recognized herself. In the past she would have chosen something so awful that the contrast between her appearance and her sisters' would have seemed deliberate, not something she had no control over.

But tonight the apprentice swan had done what she was told, and Chloe had to admit she looked pretty good—not as good as Carmen, who was petite perfection in her little black dress and big diamond earrings, but no one looked as good as Carmen. She carried their beautiful mother's genes *and* the DNA of her gorgeous birth father. Chloe had seen a picture of him once.

Before she started the car, Carmen turned to her and said, "Chloe, do you understand why Zack invited me tonight?"

"I think you're sort of a decoy."

"Right. He says his mother is crazy about you."

"No! It's just the clown connection."

"Zack says it's more than that, and I believe him. You, Chloe Kilgannon, are exactly who Bonnie Hemingway wants for the mother of her grandchildren."

Chloe swallowed hard. She wouldn't be having anyone's biological grandchildren. She would love to, but her body couldn't do the job.

"Zack thinks you're great, but—"

"I got it, Carmen. He's not about to let his mother push him into marriage, yet he's not the kind of guy who can say, 'Back off, Mom,' especially when she's celebrating her birthday.

"That's it. Zack's been a good friend, and I'm willing to help him by playing the decoy, but I'm terrible at acting. I won't be believable playing the role of prospective bride."

"Then use my motto. Keep it simple, keep it honest, and pray before you act…or in your case, try to act."

"What is it with you and prayer?" Carmen asked, exasperated. She turned on the ignition of her car and backed out of her drive very fast. "I pray for the Lord to guide my hands in surgery. I pray for Him to do what medicine can't. But I'm not going to bother God with prayers about things I should handle myself!"

"Okay, but the Bible says you're supposed to." She'd prayed for openings like this. "The Word says we're to pray about everything…all the time!"

Carmen shook her head." I don't know. Every day I see situations where God is a person's only hope. It just doesn't seem right for me to take God's time with whiny prayers about the little stuff."

"There is no 'little stuff' with God," Chloe said, unwilling to argue past that. "I'll tell you what. I'll pray that Bonnie will relax and not worry about her son. I'll pray that God gives you the words you need for tonight, and I'll pray that Zack—" What should she pray for him? "I'll pray he'll enjoy his mother's vacation as much as she does. How's that?"

Carmen shrugged her shoulders as if it didn't matter.

Lord, You gave me an opening to talk about You, and I think I blew it. If You give me another chance, I'll try to do better.

"Chloe, if you're really going to do all that praying could you throw in something about Dad's reaction when he realizes Zack and I aren't seeing each other?"

"He doesn't know that?" Chloe didn't want to be around when he found out. "Why haven't you told him? Having second thoughts?"

"No! I've *tried* to tell Dad, but he's just obsessed with Zack becoming part of our family. He's never gotten angry with me before, but I've seen how he gets with you. You can take it, but I don't have your courage."

Courage? It was more like she'd had no choice. Dad could lose his temper with her any time, any place, and she'd never known when it was coming.

"Carmen, I *can* pray that Dad takes the news calmly, but that's a very big prayer. I'll need your help with that one."

The corners of Carmen's mouth twitched. "You're probably right. Tell me what to say."

Chloe laughed out loud. "To begin with, you don't need a script. When I talked to the Lord while I was getting dressed—"

"You did that?" Carmen sounded shocked.

Chloe nodded. "I asked the Lord to keep my head straight tonight. Since neither you nor Cate fell for Zack, there's no reason to think I will, but he was all I could think about this afternoon."

"And what's wrong with that?"

"Everything. Nothing. It just makes me nervous to be this interested in a guy."

Carmen grinned knowingly. "You could always try praying that away."

Chapter Five

Zack pulled up to The Hilltop and watched his mom's face light up. High on a hill as the name suggested, the view from the restaurant was one of the best in Los Angeles. They would catch the tail end of a spectacular sunset and, later, watch the city's twinkling lights.

It was the kind of restaurant Zack's dad would have despised. He'd have griped about turning the car over to a parking valet and complained about waiting to be seated by the maître d'. When he saw the fancy menu, prices and manners of the waitstaff, he might have walked out.

Zack remembered how self-conscious he'd felt the first time he'd dined here. When the waiter had plucked the white linen napkin from the goblet and flipped it onto his lap, Zack had felt exactly like who he was—a country boy from Illinois. Tonight he took the waiter's flourish for granted and smiled when it surprised his mom.

He'd made sure she was seated at an angle so she could see the fabulous view or scan the room and perhaps see a celebrity she recognized. He'd taken the seat beside her so he could watch for Carmen and Chloe.

But Mom saw them first. "There's Chloe! Oh, my. The girls are lovely!"

Carmen looked fabulous as usual, but it was Chloe, in a terrific red dress, who made his heart rate pick up.

He stood when they approached the table. Carmen gave him a wink that said she was ready for his match-making mom. Chloe headed straight to Mom, gave her a warm embrace and said, "I've brought you a big birthday present, Bonnie. Here she is, my sister, Carmen. She's a surgeon like Zack, but *she's* ready to settle down."

Had Carmen coached her to say that? It was perfect.

Chloe stepped aside so Carmen could give Mom a pair of Hollywood air kisses and a little hug. "I have a present for you, too," Carmen said, producing an elegantly wrapped gift.

"Should I open it now?" Mom asked, already tearing the paper off.

Zack recognized the designer gift box before Mom pulled out the tiny crystal bottle of perfume.

"If you don't care for it, we can exchange it for a scent you might prefer more," Carmen said.

"Oh, no! The fragrance is lovely!" his mother exclaimed. "And it will make me think of you, Carmen."

"That's a nice gift," Chloe said, producing a small colorful bag, "but you're going to like mine better." Mom dug under the bright tissue and pulled out a red clown nose with an attached tag that read, "IOU one clown lesson and all of my 'how-to-clown' books."

His mom squealed with delight. Carmen sat beside him, and they brought her up to speed about Bonnie's clown obsession. The waiter took their drink orders, and Zack leaned back in his chair.

His mother had a birthday glow that made his heart swell with gratitude. The joy and contentment on her face was worth more than money could buy. Carmen flirted with him as planned, to throw his mother off track about his interest in Chloe.

He knew Mom had noticed him and Carmen. She'd given him a bunch of assessing looks, as if she were trying to determine if he and Carmen had more going for them than he'd claimed. Exactly what he'd hoped for.

Was he only imagining it, or was Chloe flirting with him, too? Her brown eyes sparkled with fun, and she was just so pretty he could hardly take his eyes off her. With Mom concentrating on Carmen, he didn't have to be as careful.

He noticed her sweet consideration of his mom, her quick glance of gratitude toward the waiter who filled her water glass, the way she graciously accepted her menu and her pleased expression as she looked at the menu offerings.

He hadn't thought about it, but being unimpressed with fine dining was part of the code of conduct among the rich. He'd probably adopted that attitude as well, but not Chloe. Enthusiastically, she described her favorite dishes to Mom and said this was her favorite restaurant in Los Angeles.

He'd never been this interested in a woman. He was sure of it. When his foot accidentally touched hers, his heart actually raced. Did she have any idea of how pretty she looked in that red dress? She didn't seem to, and that made him like her even more.

Chloe gripped her menu, the better to steady her nerves. What was the matter with her? She'd dined at the Hilltop so often it should feel like a second home, but she'd almost tipped over her water goblet and her salad fork had just skittered off the table and landed noisily on the hardwood floor.

It wasn't the end of the world, and Flower the Clown wouldn't have been embarrassed, but Chloe was...until Zack's dinner knife clattered to the floor, too.

With all eyes on him, he merely shrugged, smiled and said to their food server, "We seem to have flying silverware."

Had Zack copied her clumsiness to make her feel less like a klutz? Bonnie beamed at him as if she thought he had.

"You aren't worried about your reputation, Doctor?" Carmen teased. "Who's going to trust a surgeon who can't keep his silverware on the table?"

"I may have to consider a new career and enroll in Chloe's clown class," he said. "Any chance I can get Mom's rate?"

Chloe smiled to herself. She'd give him lessons for free.

They placed their orders and made small talk until their waiter served their appetizers. Bonnie looked at Zack, and without missing a beat, he said, "I'll say grace." He offered one hand to Bonnie and the other to

Carmen, who looked a little startled, but quickly followed suit. They might be the only diners holding hands while they prayed, but Chloe loved it.

Zack bowed his head and spoke in a normal conversational tone. "Lord, we praise Your name, especially on Mom's birthday, and we thank You for Your many blessings. Thank You for giving me a wonderful mother. May this next decade be the best in her long, healthy life. Bless the food, Lord, and thank You for letting us share this special occasion as family and friends."

Zack looked up to see his mom blinking back tears. He hadn't done anything that special. Maybe she was glad he still knew how to pray.

"That was a beautiful prayer, son," his mother said. "The best gift a mother can receive is knowing her child has a relationship with God."

Temporarily flushed by his mother's praise, Zack cleared the lump in his throat and said, "When I planned this dinner for you, Mom, I had no idea that your favorite conference speaker would turn out to be our new friend, Chloe, or that Chloe's sister would be my old friend, Carmen."

"*'Old?'*" Carmen protested playfully. "Watch it!"

"Sorry," he said with a grin. "It's great that such a cool coincidence brought us together."

"It *is* wonderful that we're together!" Bonnie agreed. "But I would say it was more God's direction than coincidence. When I look back over my life, I see how often I thought God wasn't hearing my prayers, but He was. Often the bad times were preparation for the good things God had ahead for me."

Zack bit his tongue as he always did when she talked about this. He loved her too much to mention she'd chosen to stay with his dad and go through those bad times. He'd finally gotten away after high school, but not without guilt because he'd left Mom to serve her sentence. That was how he thought of her life with Dad.

"I don't know what I'd do if I didn't have faith that God has my best interest at heart," Mom said, her sweet face fervent with her belief.

Carmen nodded her head in understanding. "Since Chloe's been back home, I have to confess, some of her faith is rubbing off on me." Carmen gave Chloe a sisterly squeeze on her arm.

Zack tried not to show his surprise. What was Carmen talking about? She'd always had faith—the same kind he had. It might be faith on a more generic level than his mother or Chloe seemed to have, but he believed in a Higher Power. Sometimes his patients lived when his skills hadn't been enough.

"Hey, everybody." Collin Brennan stopped by their table.

Zack stood to shake Collin's hand and whispered in his ear, "Don't mention our surgery this morning."

Collin gave him a questioning look, but blinked agreement.

"Mom," he said with a hand on her shoulder, "This is Collin Brennan, grandson of the founder of Brennan Medical Clinic where I have my office. Collin has an office there, too, and we both do our surgeries at Cedar Hills Hospital."

Color drained from her face—alarmingly so.

"I understand it's your birthday, Mrs. Hemingway, and I want to add my good wishes," Collin said with his usual charm, but he looked at Zack, silently inquiring about her sudden paleness.

"Thank you, Collin." Mom stared at Collin as if she couldn't look away.

What was wrong with Mom?

Carmen and Chloe greeted Collin like the old friends they were. Chloe leaned toward his mother and said, "Our father and Collin's uncle Albert were roommates at Stanford in their undergrad days. We've grown up together."

"Collin's an anesthesiologist, Bonnie," Carmen added. "In fact he worked with Zack this morning on their celebrity patient."

Collin gave Zack a look as if to say *he* hadn't blabbed.

"Did anyone catch Zack on TV?" Carmen asked.

"You were on TV?" his mother asked.

"When our patients are celebrities," Zack explained, "the media always wants details. Meeting with them is the worst part of my job. The cameras, the mikes in your face—I feel like a deer caught in headlights."

"And get this," Collin said, leaning down and dropping his voice, "Zack suggested that your dad, as chief of surgery, do the interview, but…our new PR guy shut your dad down."

"He didn't!" Carmen's dark eyes were wide with awe.

"Oh, but he did. The guy said, 'Dr. Kilgannon, the public needs a bright, young doctor like Dr. Hemingway to put a face to the excellence that is Cedar Hills Hospital.'"

"How did Dad take it?" Carmen asked.

Collin rolled his eyes. "If it had been anyone but Zack to take the spotlight, your dad would have stroked out, but Zack's his boy."

Zack didn't know what he'd done to gain Sterling Kilgannon's favor, but he'd had it from the moment he'd taken an office at Brennan Medical Clinic.

"Since Zack was running late, I offered to do the media interview. I *was* the anesthesiologist, and I'm a 'bright, young doctor,' but your dad said I looked too much like a soap-opera actor for the public to take seriously." Collin flashed a brilliant, TV-worthy smile. "Can you believe it?"

"Yes!" the sisters said in chorus.

"Collin, do you take after your father or your mother?" Zack's mom asked.

"I can answer that," Chloe chimed in. "Collin is blond, blue-eyed and good-looking like his dad, but he has his mother's good sense."

That was a nice way of putting it. Collin's dad was a notorious womanizer and not a man Zack could admire.

"Since it's already been on the news," Chloe said, "your patient's identity isn't confidential. May we ask who it was?"

Collin looked at Zack, clearly leaving that answer up to him.

"Madison Haines," Zack said.

"Madison Haines!" His mom almost came out of her chair. "What happened?"

"Car accident," Collin responded as if her reaction were normal. "It's been on the news. Do you follow professional golf, Mrs. Hemingway?"

"I've known Madison since he was a boy! He grew up with Zack. He still stops by when he's in town. My late husband was a golf-course superintendent. Madison worked for him and learned to play on our course."

"You didn't mention that, buddy," Collin said.

"Is Madison going to be all right?" his mother asked.

Collin nodded. "Thanks to Zack, he'll still have a career."

His mother looked at him with amazement. "I can't believe you operated on Madison, and didn't mention it to me."

"I don't normally talk about my patients, Mom."

"But Madison isn't just any patient. He sent flowers for your dad's funeral."

"You really do know him!" Collin seemed impressed.

"My husband hired Madison and Zack when the boys were in high school. Roland admired the way Madison would use every spare moment and every opportunity to improve his game, but Zack—"

"I know he didn't practice," Collin teased. "I've played with your son. His game is as bad as mine."

"Zack loved science." She smiled at Zack.

Come to think of it, she'd smiled a lot those days. His dad would be furious at him, spewing out hateful words that felt like knives, predicting Haines's success and Zack's failure, and Mom would pat his cheek, smile and say Dad didn't mean that.

"Right now, I imagine Haines and his family are very glad Zack didn't take golf seriously," Collin said. "Dr. Kilgannon told them if he were the one needing this particular surgery, he'd want Zack."

"Your dad would have been so proud," Carmen said, approval in her eyes.

The support of his friends meant a lot to Zack, but he knew the truth, and so did Mom. Nothing he had done, nothing he would ever do, would have made his dad proud. He'd gotten used to it after all those years. Hard work was its own reward and he didn't need anyone's approval.

He felt a nudge on his foot. It had to be Chloe. He risked a glance at her, and the admiration in her eyes seemed to go straight to his heart. "Good for you," she said, her eyes locking with his.

That thing about not needing approval? Normally he didn't, and he wasn't sure he did now, but approval from Chloe felt as a welcome cool breeze on a hot summer day.

Chapter Six

When Chloe and Carmen returned from dinner with the Hemingways, they found Cate in the pool behind Carmen's house, swimming laps as if her life depended upon it.

"She's been working out with clients all day, yet this is the way she relaxes," Carmen said, shaking her head in wonder.

"I heard that," Cate replied with a splutter. "Why don't you get your lazy surgical self in here and give your body a chance to do what it was meant to do? And you could add a little muscle tone, Ms. World Traveler."

For two cents, Chloe would strip out of her red dress, jump in the pool and show her mouthy little sister who had muscles and who did not. She might be a few pounds underweight, but she was half a foot taller, and she'd never lost a battle to the little blond shrimp in the pool.

"Have you learned to hold your breath longer than

you could last week, Catie baby?" she challenged as she kicked off her shoes and started to unzip her dress.

Carmen's hand snagged her arm. "Chloe! We have neighbors!"

Chloe laughed. She hadn't intended to shed her clothes, just act big and bad. Cate's grin said she knew it, too. Carmen had played the oldest sister role, right on cue.

"If you're going to make fun of me, I'm going to bed," Carmen said.

"A pajama party! That sounds like fun!" Cate swam to the side and hoisted herself out of the water. "Chloe can show me how tough she is tomorrow. After I shower, I'll make smoothies for us. I bought big, beautiful strawberries, bananas and blueberries today."

"None for me," Chloe said. "I'm stuffed from our big meal."

"Chloe, how many servings of fruit have you had today?" Cate asked, her hands on her hips. Cate had become Chloe's self-appointed health monitor. "Have you had any flaxseed at all?"

Chloe took perverse pleasure in riling her sister. It was one of the few acceptable rebellions she had left. "I guess I could nibble on a few berries…with cream and sugar."

"Sugar! Cream!" Cate cringed as she wrapped herself in a towel and padded toward her room, muttering, "And she's supposed to be the genius in the family."

Chloe picked up her shoes and smiled to herself. Living here with her sisters was such a blessing. The Lord had given Carmen a house with three bedrooms and the generosity to share it.

In her room, Chloe slipped out of her red dress and

carefully hung it in the closet. She'd loved wearing it tonight or, to be more exact, she'd loved seeing the admiration in Zack's face.

What a day this had been. It had started with her questioning why God would take away the work she loved, and it was ending with her wondering if God was giving her Zack.

Thinking of life's possibilities, she changed into a sleep outfit and ambled into the kitchen. Cate was already there. The tiny dynamo had showered, left her long honey-blond hair to air dry and gotten to work cutting fruit for her icy drinks.

Like Carmen and Mom, Cate was petite, but her daily workouts as a physical-fitness trainer made her strong. She was the only one of the sisters who'd picked up their dad's fair hair and hazel eyes, and she and Chloe were the only Kilgannons with the same skin tone—a blend of Irish and Latin genes that made them appear to have a light tan all year round.

Cate dropped the fruit into a blender, and Chloe offered to help.

"You can get the glasses and napkins. So, what did you think of Zack's mother?" Cate asked as she poured her frothy treat into three glasses.

Joining them, Carmen answered, "Bonnie Hemingway is a lovely, gracious woman with one serious flaw. She collects clowns as a hobby."

"Then she must have *loved* Chloe!" Cate took her drink and led the way to the lanai where she curled up on one end of the sofa. Carmen took the other end, and Chloe got comfortable on the chaise.

"I'm giving her clown lessons this week," Chloe said. "She was so excited."

"Aw, that's sweet," Cate approved.

Carmen rolled her eyes. "Bonnie would have wanted lessons if Chloe were a snake charmer. The woman has visions of tall, brilliant grandchildren who look like Zack and Chloe."

"And what's wrong with that?" Cate asked. "I thought you were through hoping for a love connection with Zack."

"I am! I'm just saying she's got her sights set on Chloe, and she's as subtle about her matchmaking intentions as our parents are."

"What happened to the grand plan between you and Zack?" Chloe asked. "I thought you were supposed to act as if you were his bride-to-be."

"That's what I'd like to know!" Carmen said testily. "He seemed to forget about that when he saw you tonight. That's the last time I'm doing him a favor. Cate, Zack couldn't keep his eyes off Chloe."

Cate glanced at Chloe. "Really?"

Chloe shook her head.

"Big fibber," Carmen said with a grin. "You two definitely have something going on. The only time he wasn't checking you out was when Collin Brennan stopped by."

"Collin was at the Hilltop?" Cate asked.

Carmen nodded. "And it was so strange. Zack's mother had been so outgoing, charming and pleasant, but she was borderline rude to him."

"I noticed it, too," Chloe said. "Very odd."

"I could tell it bothered Zack," Carmen said.

"It bothered him more when you mentioned his surgery on Madison Haines," Chloe said, "though you couldn't have known it would."

Carmen put her head in her hands and groaned. "I thought Zack would appreciate it if his mother knew he'd saved a pro golfer's career, but it was like I'd poured salt into an old wound. It turns out that Haines and Zack were friends in high school."

"I got the impression that it was Haines and Zack's *dad* who were friends," Chloe added dryly. "Has Zack talked much about his family?"

Carmen looked surprised. "No, and I didn't realize that until you asked. He flies home twice a year—on Bonnie's birthday and at Christmas—but his dad never visited him, and Bonnie hadn't either until this week."

"Families don't always get along," Cate observed with a sigh.

"Tell me about it," Chloe said dryly. "I called the house when I came back into town, but Mom was leaving for an appointment and hasn't called back. I haven't seen Dad, so I don't know if I've upset them, or they've just been busy. Do you two know where I stand?"

Carmen and Cate shared a telling glance.

"It's like this," Cate said slowly, as if she were choosing her words carefully. "You've gone your own way for so long that Mom thinks you don't need her. She says you're so much smarter than she is, she doesn't know how to talk to you."

Chloe didn't know what to say.

"You're very easy to talk to, Chloe," Carmen said

comfortingly. "It's not your fault that Mom measures her worth by her beauty, not her brains."

"But it's understandable that she does," Cate put in. "Dad's confirmed it for thirty years. He still treats Mom like she's the gorgeous flight attendant who brought his drink and his pillow."

"It was a different generation," Carmen argued. "Mom thought she'd made it when she became a doctor's wife. She's been content to wait on him. Dad only treats me better because we have medicine in common."

"Give me a break!" Cate threw a pillow at Carmen. "You've been his favorite daughter—make that his *only* daughter from the moment he saw you. I used to cry when he ignored me, and Mommy would say not to mind. Daddy had loved little Carmie before he even loved her."

"No need to be sarcastic, Cate," Carmen chided. "I may be Dad's favorite, but you're Mom's."

"And that leaves me…?" Chloe asked dryly.

"Better off than you realize," Carmen fired back.

"You're free to have a best friend who isn't your mother," Cate asserted.

"You don't have to worry how angry your dad will be when he realizes you're not going to marry the man of his choice," Carmen said bitterly.

"Mom is just as positive Zack's for me." Cate folded her body into a cross-legged yoga position. "Zack had barely joined Brennan Medical Clinic when everyone in our circle realized he was interested in Beth Brennan. They would have been a good match, but Dad and Mom went after that man like he was royalty or something."

"They did," Carmen agreed with weary resignation. "Chloe, you don't know how embarrassing it's been. We've tried to tell them. But Cate can't stand making Mom unhappy, and I can't take it when Dad disapproves of me. Both of us love Zack as a friend—"

"More like a brother," Cate muttered. "He gets on my nerves."

"Poor Zack," Carmen sighed. "He deserves a woman who gets butterflies in her stomach when she sees him and gets so flushed around him she can't think of a thing to say."

With that criteria, Chloe certainly qualified for the job.

"Well, I'll never marry a doctor!" Cate protested vehemently. "Especially a surgeon. I don't want a marriage like Mom's. I say it's up to Chloe."

"What about Beth Brennan?" Chloe asked. "Did Zack lose interest in her?"

"Beth married Noah, her office nurse," Carmen answered. "She's blissfully happy."

Cate cocked her head to one side and looked at Chloe with dreamy eyes. "Carmen, I'm having a vision…of Chloe…in wedding-white."

Carmen cocked her head and looked at Chloe the same way. "You're right…and Zack's beside her…both of them in wedding-white."

Chloe groaned. Why wouldn't they leave her alone?

"Oh! And we're the bridesmaids!" Cate dreamed on.

"We're wearing a pretty shade of green," Carmen said in a wistful voice.

"No, there are no pretty shades of green," Cate said, just as dreamily.

"Well, we're not in pink…or peach."

"You're right. We're in blue," Cate said, clinging to her visionary voice. "It *is* Chloe's favorite color."

"And we *do* both look good in blue."

"Then…it's settled," Cate said, her tone drifting peacefully. "We're in blue…and Chloe's in white."

Chloe got up and went to the refrigerator to see if there were more strawberries. They wouldn't even notice she was gone.

"And Zack's boutonniere will be a flower from Chloe's bouquet, while the groomsmen will wear flowers like we carry. Do you have a favorite time of year, Chloe?" Cate asked.

"Sorry, girls, but you need to work with a different bride. It's not going to be me."

That silenced her sisters for a moment.

"Is there someone else?" Cate wanted to know.

"No, but it won't be me giving Bonnie grandchildren who share her gene pool. I hate to spoil the mood, but I might as well tell you now and get it over with. A couple of years ago, my appendix ruptured when I was in Indonesia after an earthquake. Without proper treatment, infection damaged my ovaries and fallopian tubes beyond repair."

"Why didn't you tell us before?" Cate asked sympathetically.

Chloe felt a twinge of the misery she'd felt at the time.

"You've had a second opinion on that?" Carmen asked.

Chloe nodded. "Second and third. It would really

help if you didn't feel sorry for me. I know you do, but I try not to relive that disappointment, especially when there are thousands of adoptable kids who need a loving home. If I meet a man who wants to adopt, I hope I'll fall for him. If I don't, I'll adopt children on my own— as many as I can afford."

The baffled expressions on her sisters' faces reminded Chloe of all the times she'd been the odd one out, the different one, the sister who thought and lived unconventionally. Carmen and Cate would eventually marry and have children. Her life would be different.

"Just how many kids are you talking about?" Cate asked, her brow furrowed. "Am I going to have to get a second job so the kids will have birthday and Christmas presents from Auntie Cate?"

Chloe's heart turned over. "I'm not thinking double digits, Catie. When I said I'd adopt as many children as I can afford, I was factoring in my modest income."

"You are going to *try* to find a daddy for these children, aren't you?" Carmen asked worriedly.

"Well, sure. Not only would it make adopting children easier, kids *should* have a father!" Chloe was surprised that Carmen would need reassurance about the obvious. "But when do you say to a guy, 'How do you feel about adopting a big family? I don't plan to have biological children.'"

"Not on the first date, that's for sure!" Cate said, rolling her eyes.

"And if you wait until feelings develop, then he could say you led him on," Carmen reasoned. "When *is* the right time?"

"I know!" Chloe agreed. "That's why I assume I'll be a single parent. It doesn't worry me. I've taken care of children on my own for years."

Cate started laughing, just a little at first, but her laughter was contagious. Chloe smiled and giggled without knowing what was funny. It just felt good to laugh. Carmen joined them, laughing until she held her sides and asked, "What are we laughing about?"

"It's not that funny, but…" Cate had to stop when laughter stole her words again. "Zack and Chloe really are perfect for one another. Think about it. Chloe's prepared to raise children on her own, but she doesn't have the income to adopt as many kids as she wants. Zack has the income, and she won't mind if he's not at home to help raise them. Chloe, I'm not sure you'd even feel married. It's perfect."

It wasn't perfect at all. Chloe felt the burn of tears behind her eyes, though she wasn't sure why.

"And what does Zack get out of this arrangement?" Carmen asked dryly.

"A Kilgannon bride! He'll be an official Kilgannon."

In the silence that followed her words, Cate looked from one sister's sober face to the other. "You're right. I'm a twit for trying to be funny. I'm sorry."

"It's okay," Carmen said, opening her arms. "Group hug?"

Now that was a perfect idea. Chloe loved feeling so close to her sisters. She didn't know what the future would bring, but she wouldn't be alone. Her heart swelled with gratitude that the Lord had brought her home and given her this love.

Cate said softly, hesitantly, "Can I add just one thing?"

"Are you sure you want to?" Carmen asked with a warning tone.

Chloe hoped Cate's "one thing" wouldn't break this sweet, bonding moment.

"About the wedding plans—"

"Cate!" Carmen said, her warning fierce.

"But Carmen, I just want to say that our bridesmaids dresses should be pale blue, not dark blue, because dark blue washes out our complexions and—"

Carmen looked at Chloe and said, "I've got the top."

"I've got the bottom." Chloe bent to grab Cate's legs.

Whisking Cate off her feet, they headed for the pool.

"I'm right! You know I'm right!"

The shrimp didn't make that much of a splash.

Chapter Seven

Zack stood in the bathroom, shaving, wishing he were heading to the OR instead of back to the conference hotel for breakfast with Mom and then the Sunday-morning worship service. It wasn't that he minded being with his Mom. He'd looked forward to the week they'd be spending together, but the break from his routine was playing havoc with his mind.

He'd stayed awake half the night, replaying the evening with Mom, Carmen and Chloe at the Hilltop. It was normal for him to replay his surgeries, analyzing them for how he could have done better, but he didn't analyze *dinners!*

He was surprised that he couldn't get Chloe out of his mind. He'd met many pretty, intelligent women, some with a sense of humor almost as good as hers, but he'd never felt a tug on his heart the way he felt when he was with her. Chloe Kilgannon literally took his breath away.

It couldn't be real, but he could see why men followed that exhilarating feeling instead of the facts, and the fact was that he and Chloe weren't meant to be together.

She was a woman who put blind faith in God, and he was a guy whose conscience demanded that he qualify faith. Yes, God was real, and Zack may have seen more evidences of that than Chloe, but he wasn't ready to believe that everything was part of God's plan.

And then there was the matter of what each of them wanted from life. The way she loved children, he knew she'd want a big family. He wanted peace and quiet. Or so he'd thought. She'd made him think of what his future could be.

Like her sisters, Chloe would make a great friend. He wouldn't let a little one-day attraction get out of hand. Today Mom was sure to make a beeline for Chloe at the conference breakfast, but he'd have to set his mother straight.

At the conference breakfast table, Mom had saved two seats, and Zack didn't have to ask whom the other was for. It didn't matter. Chloe wasn't going to affect him today.

An hour later, he felt like a fool. He'd thought that he would be unaffected by Chloe, but sitting beside this absolutely adorable woman made him so aware of her presence he couldn't think of much else.

This morning she wore her dark hair pulled back from her face and caught at the nape of her neck. Unlike himself, she must have had a good night's sleep. Her big brown eyes snapped with good humor. She wore a white top that hinted at a figure no man would fault, and her long, slender legs were covered with tan pants.

He hadn't been paying attention to her conversation with Mom. With the three of them seated side by side at a round table for ten, it was hard to hear. But Mom leaned across Chloe to include him as she said, "Chloe, would you join Zack and me this afternoon? After the worship service, we're going to drive out to the ocean and eat at some nice restaurant on the water."

"I was thinking of the Newport Beach area," he said, not really sure if he wanted her to say yes, but positive he didn't want her to say no.

"I would love to."

It made him feel great to hear those four little words.

"But I can't."

That took the wind out of his sails!

"The conference speakers have an evaluation meeting after the worship service," Chloe explained. "I could be tied up here until mid-afternoon, and tonight is my parents' weekly Sunday-night supper. I've managed to skip it since I've been back in town, but I have orders to be there tonight. Are you two coming? I understand that you're something of a regular there on Sunday nights, Zack."

"Are we invited, Zack?" his mother asked, hope bright in her blue eyes.

"We *were* invited, but…"

"We're not going?" his mother asked with disappointment.

He hated that. The idea had been for Mom not to get her hopes up about a potential Kilgannon bride, but she'd met two of the Kilgannon sisters anyway. In retrospect, it seemed like a dumb idea. "We can go if you want to, Mom."

"Wonderful!"

"Good!" Chloe agreed, smiling herself. "You'll get to meet my sister, Cate. Collin and his wife will probably be there. You met him last night. His dad, his uncles and their wives usually show up since the Brennans are like family."

Somewhere in the middle of Chloe's remarks, his mother's face went pale as it had last night, and her smile completely vanished. Even if he hadn't been a physician, Zack would have been concerned.

"Mom, are you okay?"

She looked up at him with an imitation of her beautiful smile. "Of course, darling. I was just thinking that I might not be up for meeting a lot of people today. I think I'm more weary than I want to admit."

"Maybe a week from tonight," Chloe suggested. She glanced at him with a look that said she'd noticed that something wasn't right with Mom, too.

"That will be my last night in California," Mom said with a faraway expression. "I can do that."

Okay, Mom was scaring him. She made it sound as if she needed a full week of preparation to have supper with the Kilgannons. That wasn't like his gregarious mother.

"If you're leaving that soon, we should start those clown lessons right away," Chloe said.

"When?" his mother said, leaning forward with perky enthusiasm.

"I'm busy tomorrow," Chloe said, "but I'm available after four o'clock the next two days, and I have all day on Thursday. What would work out for you?"

Chloe glanced at Zack, and he had this silly urge to say "Every day."

"Would Tuesday be okay, darling?" his mother asked.

Tuesday would be a good start.

The conference worship service was in the hotel's ballroom. The chairs were set in rows, and Mom led the way. Zack grew more uncomfortable by the second as she passed row upon row that had three unoccupied chairs. She didn't stop until she reached the second row.

She started to lead the way into the row, but Chloe stopped her long enough to whisper something in her ear. From the way Mom waved Chloe's words away and plunged ahead to take the farthest of three seats, he guessed Chloe had offered to go in first so Mom could sit by him.

"Would you like to sit by your mother?" Chloe asked before entering the row, confirming his suspicion.

"What? And deprive Mom of matchmaking? You know what she's up to." He grinned to show he meant no disrespect to her. "If you don't mind, go ahead. Make Mom happy."

"You're a good son, Zack Hemingway."

He could be, but he wasn't sure how long he could keep it up!

Had the chairs been this close together yesterday? He could have used some more room, especially if he had any chance of concentrating on the service instead of the faint scent coming from Chloe. She smelled really good, though he couldn't place the fragrance unless it was strawberries. It might be that.

For the songs, everyone stood and sang from words on a big overhead screen. The first song was familiar and most people seemed to be singing, but not him or Chloe.

"You're not singing," she whispered.

"Neither are you," he whispered back.

"I sing like a toad."

"I sing like roadkill."

She looked up at him. "I don't know what roadkill sounds like. Sing a few bars."

Some guys couldn't resist a dare. He could.

"C'mon, sing for Jesus." She knew how to push buttons.

"You first."

She gave him an assessing look, then stared at the words on the big screen for a few seconds before opening her mouth. "Amazing Grace" came out quite recognizably. Her voice was low pitched, but not bad at all.

He bent his head close. "You don't sound like a toad."

"I'm singing for Jesus," she said, looking straight ahead.

He'd been in the male chorus in high school and some days, he sang in the shower. It just felt strange to sing when he knew others could hear him. Nevertheless, he sang along with her.

She raised her head slowly, looking at him with new respect. "You're pretty good."

He was not going to let a little praise go to his head. But he had to wonder. What else could Chloe get him to do?

Zack had planned to sleep late on his first official vacation day, but he woke at five as he did every day without the benefit of an alarm clock. Another surgeon was covering for him this week, but he showered and shaved as usual.

Pulling on a T-shirt and a pair of shorts, he headed to the kitchen to make coffee, but Mom had beaten him to it. The coffee was made and she had a mug in her hand while she read her Bible on the balcony.

He poured himself a mug of coffee and joined her. "You're up early," he said, kissing her forehead.

"Not really. I'm still on Illinois time."

"That's right! No wonder you were fading when we got home yesterday."

"But I wouldn't have changed a minute of it. Getting to see Chloe again at the conference breakfast started the day off perfectly. Then seeing the ocean and watching the sun set made it a wonderful day! I can't believe I let so many years go by without seeing the ocean."

"Why did you? I tried and tried to get you and Dad to come out for a visit."

"Your dad hated California. You know what a fuss he put up about you attending college out here."

"But I had a scholarship, and Stanford is one of the best schools in the country. It was your alma mater."

"I know. Maybe he thought he was losing you."

Dad *had* lost him, but it had happened long before Stanford.

"You know what I'd like to do today?" Mom asked brightly. As predictable as a heartbeat, she'd maneuvered them past the elephant in the room.

"What would you like, Mom? It's as good as done."

"I'd like to follow you around in your regular workday."

That seemed easy enough.

"I want go with you to the hospital, the dry cleaners, the place you work out, your church, anywhere."

"A mini-tour of my life?"

She laughed happily. "Yes! Then when we talk on the phone, I'll be able to imagine where you've been and what you've done."

"How soon can you be ready?"

"Is what I'm wearing okay?"

Her white slacks and pink top were perfect for a late April day in L.A. "You look great. I'll be ready in five minutes."

"Should I make breakfast?"

"Not if we're going to follow my daily schedule."

"Then I'll just get my purse."

Zack clipped his security ID to his blue polo-shirt pocket and said, "Our first stop should be the doctors' lounge. That's where I normally trade my suit jacket for a lab coat, but since I'm on vacation, we can skip that part."

"Oh, no," his mom said. "I want to see you in your lab coat."

He held the lounge door open for her.

"I can go in there?"

"It's a unisex area."

"Good morning, Bonnie!" Carmen said on her way out of the lounge. She stopped to give his mother a hug. "It's nice to see you again."

"Oh, my dear, you look lovely."

Unless she was in surgery, Carmen always dressed in a trendy outfit, heels and a trimly fitted lab coat. "Thank you," she said. "So do you. I understand you're clowning with Chloe tomorrow."

"I am, at your house."

"Zack! This must be your mother!" Dr. Albert Brennan, the man Zack had most wanted Mom to meet, stopped and took her hand. "Mrs. Hemingway, we've waited a long time to meet you."

"Thank you," Mom said, beaming. "It's wonderful to meet Zack's friends."

Mom was impressed by Albert, as Zack had known she would be. Immaculately groomed with thinning hair and very blue eyes behind rimless eyeglasses, Albert was almost as tall as Zack and almost as fit.

"Mom, you've heard me talk about Dr. Albert Brennan many times. He's been my mentor and opened many doors for me. We share an office suite at Brennan Medical Clinic."

"Yes, Zack has often talked about you," Mom said, in her usual gracious way, but healthy color drained from her face.

"Mom, are you all right?"

"What? Yes, of course."

"Have you eaten breakfast, Mrs. Hemingway?" Albert asked.

"I'm giving Mom a tour of the hospital, and breakfast in the cafeteria is our next stop." Zack took his mother's arm and guided her toward the elevator.

"Could I accompany you?" Albert asked.

"We don't want to impose on your time," his mother replied.

"No imposition at all." He took her other arm. "Zack's told us you were a premed student at Stanford before you married and moved to the Midwest."

"Yes, I wanted to be a pediatrician," Mom said. "I love children."

"But you became a biology teacher?"

"Yes. Like so many women my age, I married before I finished college. After I had Zack, I earned my bachelor's and, later, my master's, but the closest medical school was a long commute. I had a son to take care of."

In the elevator, Albert punched the button for the garden level. "I met Zack when I guest-lectured at Stanford and he was a premed student. Zack reminded me of a relative of mine when that young man was Zack's age. In fact, you could say he was the spitting image."

Albert hadn't mentioned that before. What relative would that be?

"I thought Zack must surely be a long-lost member of our family, and I determined that we would stay in touch. In a way, he's become the son that my wife and I never had." Albert was looking at Mom, but she stared straight ahead, as if she were trying to tune him out.

Okay, what was going on? His mother was never like this. He looked at Albert as if to ask "Do you think my mother's ill?"

Albert shook his head. The elevator door opened and Albert punched the button for the surgical floor. "Zack, get your mother a nice breakfast. I'm running a little late. We'll get acquainted another time."

Mom let him leave without saying a word. That wasn't like her at all.

The elevator door closed, and he and Mom were alone. "Mom, I am seriously worried. Are you on some medication? Have you seen your doctor? Do you have a condition you haven't told me about?"

"I had a checkup not long ago, and I'm fine, darling." And she did look it once again. "Do you think they'll have crisp bacon? I don't eat bacon anymore because of the nitrates, but I'd love it as a vacation treat."

Bacon? Vacation treat? "Mom, I'd like to have a col-league run you through some tests."

"Whatever for? I'm probably the healthiest sixty-year-old you know."

"Humor me? Just see the doctor?"

"What doctor?"

Good question. Which of Brennan Medical Clinic's excellent physicians should they begin with?

"Just a doctor from the clinic, Mom. If you want to see what I do in a normal day, then a tour of Brennan Medical Clinic is on our agenda anyway."

"When you say 'tour,' what exactly do you have in mind, Zack?"

"The building itself is impressive, as is the lobby. We could have coffee or lunch in the dining area. I want my staff to meet you, and my friends and of course the Brennans."

"That sounds lovely," she said, not meeting his eyes. "Of course I want to visit the clinic, but it seems a waste of all this California sunshine to stay indoors today. Could we drive around and see where you play instead of where you work?"

"It's early. We could do both."

"How about a tour of Universal Studios? That sounds like fun."

"That's mostly indoors, Mom. No California sunshine."

"It still sounds like fun."

He wished they'd set up Mom's clown lesson for this afternoon instead of tomorrow. He knew she wouldn't change her mind about that.

And the bonus would have been that he would have gotten to see Chloe sooner. Tomorrow afternoon seemed like a long time to wait.

Chapter Eight

Zack sat in front of his TV with the sound turned low, not really watching the baseball game, but wishing it would distract him from worrying about Mom. The time-zone difference had finally caught up with her and she'd gone to bed early, leaving him with too much time to wonder what was wrong with her.

He needed a friend right now, but who could he talk to? Collin and Albert would have been his first choices, but he'd begun to wonder if Mom's episodes weren't somehow related to them. Carmen had bowed out of his life. He barely knew Chloe, but she knew Mom better than anyone else in L.A.

He took his cell phone and went out to his car. If Mom should wake, he wouldn't want her to hear his conversation. He didn't have Chloe's phone number, but Carmen was on speed dial. She answered on the second ring.

"How was your day?" he began, feeling awkward

about them being friends, yet he'd called to talk to her sister.

"Do you want to talk to Chloe?" she asked, bypassing the small talk.

It was too embarrassing to admit it. "What makes you think that?"

"Well, it's not because I'm psychic. Do you want to talk to her or not?"

"Sure. I'll talk to her for a while."

Carmen burst out laughing, but she called out, "Chloe, the phone's for you."

And then Chloe was on the phone. "Zack?"

He felt better just hearing her voice. "Hi."

"How did your day with your mom go?"

"That's why I called. I'm worried about her."

"Where are you?"

It wasn't a response he'd expected. "In my car outside my condo. I'm pretty sure Mom's crashed for the night, but I couldn't be sure."

"Why don't you come over?"

"Really?"

"You're not that far away."

That was true, and he would like to see her. "How about your sisters? I'd rather not share—"

"We can talk in your car."

He put his key into the ignition. "I'll be there in ten minutes."

It was less than that when he turned into Carmen's drive, but Chloe was waiting. His car headlights picked up Chloe, barefoot, her hands in the back pockets of her jeans, her legs in a ready stance. Her long straight hair lay on one shoulder, and her expression said she could handle anything.

Just seeing her made him feel better.

He reached over and opened the passenger door for her. "I'm sorry to barge in on your evening," he began, his brow furrowed.

"We're friends. Barging is allowed. So what's up?" She turned her body toward him and crossed her long legs. He shifted to face her.

Ambient light from the house and the street provided enough light for him to read her features, but he still had the feeling of them being very alone.

A swath of her hair fell across her face and she reached up to tuck it behind her ear. His eyes followed the action.

"You have beautiful hair, Chloe."

"Thank you. So do you." She looked stricken. "Forget I said that. Men don't want to be told that."

"What makes you think that?" he asked, wanting to laugh.

"I read the manual. It was in Cate's room. A magazine really, but it had articles on what a man really wants."

Okay, that was funny, but she was serious about this. "I would say you look great tonight, but you've got to promise you won't say I do, too."

Chloe was sufficiently embarrassed that she didn't plan to say much at all. She looked down at her old comfortable clothes and bare feet, and then looked at him in his designer jeans and T-shirt that probably had a designer label as well. "Actually, you look better than me…but only because you're wearing shoes."

Smiling, he said, "There will never be a time I'll look better than you."

Her first instinct was to argue the point, but wouldn't that make her sound as if she were fishing for compliments?

"You're a very pretty woman, Chloe Kilgannon."

Had one of her sisters told him how self-conscious she was about her lack of good looks? "No makeup tonight," she said, running a finger across her face.

"Still, very pretty," he said with his big smile, the one that gave her a chill.

"On the way over here, I kept asking myself why I felt I had to talk to you."

"Did there have to be a reason?"

"For me, yes. I'm analytical to a fault."

"As bad as Carmen?"

"Oh, way worse than Carmen! You always make me laugh. That's a reason. But a better one is that I knew you'd help me figure out what's been going on with Mom."

He couldn't have given her a better compliment. "Tell me what you think is wrong."

"That's just it. I can't put it into words. One minute Mom is her usual happy self, the next minute I think I should rush her to an ER."

"No wonder you're worried!"

"I told Mom a doctor should see her, but she claimed she'd had a physical recently and insisted she was fine. Chloe, did Mom look fine to you at the conference Saturday?"

"Yes, definitely."

"I agree. How about at the Hilltop?"

"Let's see. She looked fine before Collin Brennan stopped by and she was fine after he left. Carmen and I both noticed it."

"Then I wasn't imagining it. Did you notice her do the one-eighty switch any other time?"

Since he wasn't leading her, she had to think for a moment. "At the conference breakfast, we were talking about Mom and Dad's Sunday supper. Bonnie was excited about going…and then she turned ashen and said she was too tired. Is that what you're talking about?"

"Exactly, but she was perky enough to play matchmaker at the worship service, and she was full of energy the rest of the day. So I ask myself, what's suppressing the temporary blood flow and what's causing the mood swings? Is it physiological, psychological, what?"

"Could it have been anything we said Sunday morning?"

Zack closed his eyes, "Let me think about it."

Chloe watched him think for a while before she closed her own eyes and listened to the palm fronds rustling in the night. The quiet was no help to Chloe's memories of Bonnie, but Zack would be memorable for some time to come.

Cate said he worked out, not for vanity's sake, but to keep his body strong for long hours in the E.R. Whatever the reason, he had great shoulders, biceps and forearms. And she should be checking out the stars instead of the guy.

"On Sunday morning, we were talking about Mom meeting your family and friends," he said thoughtfully.

"And today's episode?"

"Mom and I were at the hospital doctors' lounge," he said, running his hand through his short hair as if it helped him to think. "Carmen came out and said hello. Albert Brennan came out and said nice things about me. And somewhere in there, Mom lost both color and energy. It was like her blood sugar took a dive…but then she was better when we were alone again."

"For the rest of the day?"

"She didn't lose color again, but sometimes she seemed lost in thought. That's not like Mom. If I insist on tests, it will ruin her vacation, but if I don't…"

His voice trailed off, but Chloe understood. Any doctor would feel bad about a missed diagnosis, but if the patient were a parent, it would be unthinkable.

"Mom's only been here since Friday night. She leaves a week from today. If there's something wrong, I'd like to know what it is before I let her go."

She wanted to take his hand and say something comforting. That was what she would have done with someone she knew better. Why should he be any different just because he could make her heart beat faster? He still was a friend in need. She touched his hand.

His eyes went to her hand and then to her face as if he were surprised. But he took her hand and laced his fingers with hers, clasping and re-clasping as if he were searching for the perfect fit. He must have found it because he pulled her hand to his chest.

She felt him take a long, deep breath, and he seemed to relax as he breathed out. "Thank you. I knew I'd feel better, talking with you."

"Any time. Any day."

"I'll see you tomorrow at Mom's clown lesson?"

"It's a date. Can't wait."

He laughed, kissed her fingers and released her hand. "There's nobody like you, Chloe. Nobody at all. See you tomorrow."

When the doorbell rang late Tuesday afternoon, Chloe jammed on a red clown nose and opened the door, breathlessly ready to see Zack and his mother.

But Bonnie was there alone, and Zack stood by his car in the drive. "When you and Mom are finished, give me a call. I'll come back for her."

"Okay, but you're welcome to stay. You don't have to participate."

"Sure, you say that now," he said with a grin, "but I've seen you in action."

"What if I promise to be good?"

"That's tempting," he said, looking very tempting himself in his sleeveless gray T-shirt and dark running pants. "But it's too nice to be indoors. I'm going for a run. See you later."

She didn't want him to leave. She'd redone her makeup and hair! She'd put on a feminine skirt, a blouse and earrings! He'd held her hand last night and kissed it. What had she missed?

"Well, that makes my day," Bonnie said happily. "You're disappointed that he didn't stay! Chloe, darling, that means you're developing feelings for Zack. If it wouldn't shock your neighbors, I would dance on your doorstep."

"This is L.A., Bonnie. You could dance in the street wearing your pj's and nobody would notice."

"Well done! You neither confirmed or denied, which leaves the prospective mother-in-law wondering."

"Bonnie, you don't hold anything back, do you?" Chloe said, loving this funny lady who made it plain what she wanted. "Come on in."

"I brought you a present." Bonnie handed her a colorful bag.

"How pretty! Everyone says, 'you shouldn't have,' but I love presents!"

"Good! I can't wait for you to open it! I hope you don't already have this. I want to be the one to give it to you."

The gift was protected by so much bubble wrap and tape that Chloe needed a knife to cut through the wrapping. It was worth the trouble. The gift was a little clown figurine holding a bouquet of balloons. It was so small it fit into Chloe's hand, and the detailing was exquisite, from the clown's sweet face to her costume with two big buttons and a ruffled collar.

"Bonnie, this is adorable. I love it!"

"Then you don't already own it?"

"No, but my mother collects this designer's figurines. I know what an extravagant gift this is, and I don't know what to say! *Thank you* doesn't seem enough."

"I thought the little clown could be me." Bonnie's eyes were bright with hope. "See the buttons on his little clown suit. I thought my name could be Buttons, and I could learn to pull buttons from behind children's ears or play a simple game like Button, Button, Who's Got the Button?"

"It's a great idea!"

"The buttons will have to be big enough that small children won't swallow them or put them up their little noses. I thought I could attach buttons to my hat, my shoes and a big ring that I'd wear on top of my gloves."

"Your ideas are wonderful. All we need to do is design your makeup."

They worked on Bonnie's makeup, practiced some tricks and discussed the do's and don'ts of clowning. Chloe gave Bonnie books to take home for reference.

"I probably should call Zack to come get me," Bonnie said when a couple of hours had passed. "I want him to see me in my clown makeup."

Chloe started putting her clown things away. After Bonnie made her call, she helped tidy the room.

"Chloe, what comes after your work with Love Into Action?"

"I'm learning I can adjust to anything that I sense is God's will. Recognizing it is the hard part."

Bonnie sighed. "And when you choose a path that you think is right, but it isn't, it's so hard, even impossible, to find another way. I chose poorly as a young adult and paid for it dearly."

Curiosity made Chloe wonder, but she wouldn't ask.

"Five years from now, what do you see in your life, Chloe? What do you want most?" Bonnie had a knack for digging into one's heart with such finesse that it didn't seem intrusive.

"Five years from now? My testimony of working with children around the world will be old news. I'll be in less demand as a speaker. What will I be doing? What do I want most? Good questions, Bonnie. The Word says we're to ask specifically for what we want. The Lord loves to give us our heart's desire."

"Spoken like a born teacher," Bonnie said, nodding her approval. "You have the gift, Chloe. I think you'll be in demand as a speaker longer than you think. Is that what you want most?"

No, what she wanted most was to love and be loved. Sometimes she felt as if she had so much love stored away she couldn't stand it. Freely, she'd spent it on children who needed it badly, but that was yesterday. Who'd want her love five years from now?

The doorbell rang. "That must be Zack!" Bonnie went to the door.

Chloe could see herself loving Zack five years from now, but she was way ahead of herself. She went to the door, drilling home an old truth: she couldn't get hurt if she didn't care.

Zack stood at the door, freshly sun-kissed, his T-shirt a little damp with sweat and his blue eyes bluer than ever.

"Hi," he said simply with his brilliant smile.

With no words available, she could only smile back.

"Is Mom ready?"

"I am," Bonnie said, "but I could use some help with all I have to carry."

"Okay if I come in?" he asked.

He'd had to ask? Where were her manners? She stood aside.

"Nice makeup, Mom, or should I call you something else? I know how particular you clowns are about names." He gave Chloe a teasing glance that sent a little thrill along her spine.

"If I had the rest of my costume on, I'd be Buttons. Of course if I had the costume on, I couldn't tell you that. We clowns don't talk."

"I know! So, you went with Buttons. Good. I like that."

"Zack was with me when I shopped for your gift," Bonnie clarified.

"I love it," Chloe said, trying to think of him as a fellow clown's son…not a man to build a dream on.

"Did you have a nice run?" Bonnie asked, loading Zack with the books, a costume and clown accessories.

"The sun was really hot, but there was a good breeze. Did you learn everything you need to know? Are you ready to clown with Chloe at the hospital?"

"Not yet. I need to practice my tricks before I'm ready to hit the stage."

"I didn't have *any* practice when Chloe dragged me on stage."

"That was Flower who did that," Chloe stated loftily. "And if you're part of the audience, practice is not required."

Out came his smile, the big one, the one that made her weak in the knees.

"From the looks of all this stuff you're taking home," he said, "I think we owe Chloe for dinner. What do you think, Mom?"

Chloe's heart slammed hard against her chest.

"Chloe, would you have dinner with us?" Bonnie said wistfully with her dimpled smile.

Who could say no to that look?

Chapter Nine

Bonnie leafed through a tourist guidebook while she and Chloe waited for Zack to shower and change. "This ad says that Olvera Street's taquitos are the best anywhere," Bonnie said. "Is that far from here, Chloe?"

"It's in downtown L.A., but it's not too far."

"We have great Mexican restaurants in our area. You wouldn't think so since we live on the Mississippi River west of Chicago, but I don't think the taquitos at Olvera Street could be any better than we get at Adolph's in East Moline."

"Maybe not. People enjoy Olvera Street because they get that south-of-the-border ambience without driving all the way to Tijuana."

Zack joined them, wearing a T-shirt, khaki pants and sneakers. Her first impression was that this was a much better look on him than the suit and tie he'd worn at the conference; her second impression was that he'd turn heads whatever he wore.

"We're going to Tijuana?" he asked, checking his watch. "Mom, you'll fall asleep on the way back."

"No, darling, just to downtown L.A. Chloe says Olvera Street is a fun place to hang out."

"She's right," he said, ushering them out of his condo and into his car.

Chloe immediately climbed into the spacious back seat of his Mercedes coupe. She'd had a turn in the front seat last night, and back here she could put on her sunglasses and watch the driver to her heart's content.

Zack wore sunglasses, too, and she couldn't tell if he was checking her out or not, but she ought to assume she meant nothing more to him than his mother's clown tutor.

The sun was still bright when they finished their taquitos, guacamole, chips and pico de gallo. Bonnie had loved their outdoor umbrella table, the festive garlands of paper cutouts that flew overhead and the mariachi band. Loyally, she pronounced the food good, but not better than Adolph's or LaFlama back home.

From their table they could see tourists bargaining for Mexican imports in the marketplace, and Chloe could tell that Bonnie was itching to be one of them.

"What's your pleasure, ladies?" Zack asked. "For dessert they have fresh tropical fruit if you need a healthy fix after eating that much fried food. I'm going all the way. I'm having fried ice cream."

"We have that at home," Bonnie said. "A scoop of ice cream in a flour tortilla, deep fried and liberally coated with sugar…and a sprinkle of cinnamon."

"The cinnamon has healthy properties, Mom," Zack said with a wry smile. "Better go with that."

"I'm having what the doctor orders," Chloe teased, happy to see Zack relaxed and settling into his week of vacation.

"I can't eat another bite!" Bonnie said, "but I'll try it next time."

"We probably won't be back," Zack said sadly, but anyone could tell he was teasing his mother. "L.A. is a big place with lots of sights to see—Universal Studios, L.A.'s famous Farmers Market, Disneyland, Wilshire Boulevard, the Getty, the ocean—"

"Stop! Too many choices! Save some for my next visit."

"Chloe, do you have to work tomorrow?" Zack asked. "We'd love to have you go with us—wherever that is."

And she'd love to go with them. Any time with Zack was well spent, though she had to remember she was here as a friend of his mother.

"I wish I could be with you tomorrow," she said regretfully, "but I'm in the office Monday through Friday until three—except when I'm scheduled for a weekend seminar. Then I get Thursdays and Fridays off, but most of Friday is spent getting to the destination city. This Friday it's Denver."

"So, you could join us Thursday?" Zack asked.

Chloe nodded.

"Have you been to Solvang?"

"Several times. It's a charming little town."

"Mom, Solvang was settled by Danes. You ought to feel at home."

"Chloe, my father's parents were immigrants from Denmark. My maiden name is Jorgensen."

"Would you like to go to Solvang with us this Thursday?" Zack looked at Chloe hopefully.

"I'd love to go."

"Wonderful! We'll do it." Bonnie rose from the table. "While you two fast-metabolizing young people indulge one more time, I'm going to take a stroll and check out the shopping."

"Mom, wait," Zack said, pulling his wallet out. "I'll pay the bill, and we'll go with you. I don't like the idea of us getting separated."

His mother lifted one eyebrow and narrowed her eyes in a look that would have made Chloe back down. "Zackary, this is not such a big place that I can't find my way back. The day I can't shop a little on my own is the day I'll stay home."

There were times when Bonnie with the dimpled smile looked as if she needed to label her salt and pepper shakers to tell which was which, but this Bonnie took nonsense from no one.

A smile hovered on Zack's lips. "Yes, ma'am."

"Do you want to synchronize watches?" his mother asked with an edge of sarcasm. "I can be back at any agreed-upon time."

"Take as long as you like." He leaned back in his chair, as if he knew who was the boss.

Her sweet smile popped out like sunshine after rain. "Maybe I'll bring you back a treat."

"The candy shops sell a sugary fudge called *jamoncillo* that's delicious," Chloe suggested.

"No candy for me, Mom, but I'd like one of those supersized sombreros. Get two. You can wear one back on the plane."

"Maybe I will." She turned and was soon lost in the crowd of tourists.

Zack vigilantly scanned the crowd. "Do you think Mom will be all right on her own?"

"The LAPD has a presence here. I think Bonnie's safe."

"I think so, too, or I would have gone with her." He signaled their waiter and ordered their desserts.

"Where do you think you'll take Bonnie tomorrow?"

"Anywhere she wants," he said. "I want her to have the time of her life."

"Your mother is very special to you."

"Very. I loved my dad when I was little, and he was a good dad, but somewhere around junior high…I don't know what happened. He was angry with me a lot."

"People often bring their anger from the workplace home."

"Yes, they do, but Dad loved being superintendent of the golf course. As I grew older, I realized that he really hated the idea of me becoming a doctor."

"That seems strange."

"Tell me about it! Mom would say it was only because he wanted me to be a professional golfer like Haines hoped to be. I had a little talent for the game. I might have had a chance, but you need to love it like Haines did. I wanted to be a surgeon."

"But for your dad to be angry about that is…" The words *cruel, demeaning, ridiculous* all came to mind.

"You know how kids' minds work, so you'll appreciate this. I used to wonder if Haines and I got switched at the hospital, that Dad knew it and had to raise the wrong kid."

Zack was a brilliant man. He would have been a very smart kid. For him to have believed that would have been so hurtful.

"Mom would say Dad felt bad because I didn't take advantage of what he could give me—a chance to practice and be somebody famous."

"But you did! When Madison's family asked for the best, you were it!"

"It's funny how life turns out," he said, giving his attention to the waiter and the desserts placed before them.

Then he was done talking about his family. "This is totally decadent," she said, her mouth full of rich ice cream and crunchy, sweet tortilla. "Cate would have a fit if she saw us ingesting all this fat."

He laughed softly. "We'd hear about it, that's for sure. But I admire how true she is to what she believes. All three of you Kilgannon women are like that. Carmen is single-minded about her work, and loving kids is your life."

He had them figured out very well.

"Am I crossing a line if I ask what brought you back to L.A.? At dinner Friday night, you cited medical reasons for giving up your work around the world. As a physician, I couldn't help but wonder if you'd explored all treatments."

Did she want to talk about this with Zack?

"If I'm getting too personal..." He let his voice drift off, giving her the option of changing the subject.

"I had dengue fever." She blurted it out before she could change her mind.

"When, where, how bad?" he asked as if she'd reported on her ice cream.

"Three months ago. Nicaragua. Bad enough that the doctors said I might die if I got it again, or the more violent form, dengue hemorrhagic fever."

He put down his spoon and pushed his dessert away. "It's not a disease to be ignored. Mosquitoes that carry dengue fever aren't prevalent in the U.S., but they are in many of the countries where you've worked. People do die from it."

"The administrators of Love Into Action said the same thing. They sent me home for good."

"Bravo to them!"

"But I wanted to stay. I still wish I had a job that would let me hug children every day and do work where I'm needed."

"Who says you're not needed here?"

"The Lord wants me to eat ice cream with you instead of helping children who've lost everything?"

He lifted his shoulders in a playful shrug. "If God's moving you into a new phase of life, there's bound to be pitstops along the way. In the big race of life, you need time to fuel up, change your tires...eat ice cream."

As a philosopher, he wasn't half-bad. Smiling, she asked, "Why aren't you eating *your* ice cream?"

"A few bites of dessert is all I ever want. You know, I've never talked to anyone who's had dengue fever. What was it like?"

"What was it like?" she repeated, thinking of how to

describe her suffering. "It was like the worst flu imaginable, and it went on for weeks. I asked the Lord to let me die. I was so weak I couldn't have hugged a child."

"That's pretty weak," he said sympathetically.

Surprisingly, she didn't mind the sympathy. "The thing is, I'd brought this grief on myself. I was *told* to wear long pants. I was *told* to wear long-sleeved shirts and insect repellent, but the heat and humidity were so uncomfortable. I put on cooler clothes and expected the Lord to protect me. Later, lying in bed week after week, I realized He had *tried* to protect me."

Zack looked puzzled.

"I was told what to do so I wouldn't get bitten. That could have been God giving His voice to my supervisors. I didn't listen. I did it my way, and it cost me the work I loved."

His eyes seemed to look straight into her heart. "I can only imagine how I would feel if I knew I couldn't operate again," he said. "Is it like that for you?"

"Not quite, because I believe I will 'operate again,' only in some new venue."

"That's good. It's when a person loses hope that there's cause for real concern. How are you feeling these days?"

"I'm almost back to my former strength."

His eyes looked her over from head to toe. "When was the last time you had a doctor check you out?"

"About three seconds ago."

He threw his head back and laughed so loud people turned and stared. Still chuckling, he said, "You might want to get a second opinion, but this doctor thinks you look great!"

Approval like that could go to her head.

She'd have to thank her sisters. They knew how to make the most of her looks. The red skirt that flared around her knees had been Cate's choice, and the black top that made her feel so feminine had been Carmen's. Chloe's only contribution had been clasping her dark hair at the nape of her neck and wearing the silver hoop earrings she'd purchased in a little Peruvian marketplace, much like the one here.

It really helped to think of clothes and world travel instead of how much she liked being with this great guy.

The waiter came with the bill. Zack perused it, gave the young man his credit card and said, "If you have customers waiting for this table, we can leave."

"No, that's fine, señor. It's almost closing time. The street shuts down at seven."

"That's good to know. Mom will have to return."

Chloe checked her watch. "She hasn't been gone that long."

"Mom the Matchmaker. If she's a little overt about it, blame it on inexperience. She's never tried this before."

"Is she more subtle than *my* matchmaking parents?"

"You've heard about that? Cate and Carmen have never been more than good friends to me."

"My parents have had two years to send you to the altar. What does your mom expect to happen in a few days?"

"I suppose I could ask you to 'go steady.' Wasn't that the next step in our parents' day? I could give you my class ring."

"I could wear it on a chain around my neck."

He grinned. "She might like that! I think she'd like

anything symbolic that she could tell her friends about. Seriously, I know Mom's frustrated that I don't have a love life. Her friends have adult children with marriages, homes and babies. I don't blame her for wanting that, too."

"Her goal may be as simple as wanting to see that you are well loved."

He frowned as if he were thinking about it seriously.

Chloe prayed silently that Zack would be at peace with his mother's motives and know the right thing to do or say to ease her mind.

"I think I've got it," he said, chuckling. "Mom's into sightseeing. Let's head to Vegas and an Elvis wedding chapel."

"Who? The two of us?" Was he crazy?

"No, the three of us!" Zack leaned back in his chair, the very picture of a good-looking man up to no good. "Mom could take our pictures at a variety of wedding venues. She could take them home and say she helped us look for the perfect place to get married. What do you think?"

"Since it wouldn't be for real, I think she'd rather go to Disneyland."

"What if it were for real?" He leaned forward in his chair.

With his blue eyes fixed so intensely on her, Chloe couldn't breathe. "I'm not sure what you mean."

"Believe me, I don't know either. I was a steady, level-headed guy until three days ago. Now, everything's a possibility. I think it's because—"

"Vacation!" she said before he could utter another

word. "You're in vacation mode. A little time away from your routine opens up the world."

He leaned back and grinned. "Sure, that explains it."

Chapter Ten

Zack's mother returned before he could say anything that he might regret. Vacation mode—what a cool explanation of his momentary lapse in judgment. Chloe was not only smart and funny, she was wise. He really might be falling for her, but he wouldn't say so again.

For Chloe, Mom brought back *jamoncillo*. For herself, she'd purchased hand-dipped candles. He got a pat on the cheek which had always been Mom's favorite gesture.

With the restaurant and stores shutting down on Olvera Street, they had no choice but to walk back to his car.

"What can we do now, kids?" Bonnie asked.

"There are shops and amusement rides at the beaches," Chloe suggested.

"I think I'm shopped out today," his mom said. "What could we do that doesn't involve more walking?"

"There's more to do at the beach than shop," he said. "We could watch the sun set and the moon come up."

"Oh!" his mother happily exclaimed. "I haven't done

that since I was a student at Stanford. Is that okay with you, Chloe?"

"I'd like that." She gave him a look and for his ears only murmured, "Better than a road trip to Vegas."

The sky was a golden glory when Zack let his mother off near the sand. She sped off to save the perfect spot for their blanket, or so she said.

"Bonnie makes a fast exit," Chloe said as he pulled away to find a parking spot. "How can she have a health problem and move like that?"

"I know."

"Did she have any of her 'episodes' today?"

"Not one. This morning I took her downtown to the garment district so she could shop for bargains—her favorite sport. Then, she had her clown lesson and she's been fine ever since."

He parked the car and Chloe helped him unload the purchases he'd made on the way to the beach—a couple of blankets, a Thermos of hot chocolate, bottled water and some other stuff he'd thought they might need.

"How long are you planning for us to stay?" Chloe teased.

He grinned. "I like to be ready for anything."

"This is a lot of stuff, but I doubt that it will prepare you for anything. Your mom carries a big bag of tricks."

"You've noticed? For the record, I can't think of another woman I'd rather have as a partner in Mom's matchmaking game."

"I'm a little concerned about Bonnie's expectations.

She doesn't think we're going to fall for each other while she's here, does she?"

"I don't know. She and my dad got married a week after she came home from college, and they'd never dated before. Could you fall for a guy in less than a week?"

"I wouldn't want to," she said honestly. "I'd want a courtship—flowers, candy, the whole nine yards." That wasn't exactly how she felt, but Cate's manual was very clear. Men liked "the chase." Once the guy caught the girl, it could be over.

At the perfect spot on the beach chosen by his mom, Chloe took one of the blankets, whipped it into the air and guided it across the sand. She used her shoes to anchor two corners of the blanket. Zack kicked off his sneakers and anchored the other two corners.

When he turned around, Chloe was on her knees, draping the second blanket around Mom. It was a simple kindness, but it touched his heart.

"Back in Illinois, we have beautiful sunsets," Mom said. "But this? I feel as if I'm right in the middle of it."

"I know!" Chloe's enjoyment of the good in life set her apart from other women he'd known, and her smile seemed as bright as the sunset. He'd never known anyone who took such pleasure in the moment.

Mom sat on the left side of the blanket facing the ocean, and Chloe scooted over to the far right, leaving him room to sit by Mom. The way Chloe huddled on the edge of the blanket, she was almost in the sand.

He reached over and pulled her a little closer. "Mom won't like it if you're off by yourself," he said into her ear.

The crashing waves made small talk difficult, but they all seemed to be content to sit quietly and watch the sun slip below the horizon. Soon it was cooler and the breeze picked up. Chloe tucked her legs under her skirt.

"Zack, this blanket's big enough for all three of us if we cuddle in," Mom said. She kept an end for herself and passed the rest for him to share with Chloe.

"You heard Mom, Chloe," he said softly. "Cuddle in."

Chloe looked up at him and rolled her eyes, but she moved in so close he could smell that faint fragrance she wore. Strawberries, that was what it smelled like, and he'd always loved strawberries.

"If we link our arms together," Mom said, matching words to action, "our body heat will keep us very comfortable."

As the physician among them, he could say they didn't need the arm linkage for the short time they would be here, but when Chloe followed directions, it felt pretty great. Was Chloe feeling the connection, too?

He looked down, hoping their eyes would meet, but she was looking at the sky as if she hoped to spot the first star. When her body began to shake, his medical instincts fired. Was she sick?

A quick glance settled him down. Chloe's ailment was only suppressed laughter.

"I've changed my mind," she said, looking at him.

He could hardly hear her over the sound of the ocean. Lowering his head, he said, "And?"

"I underestimated your mother. Big time. She might have booked a wedding chapel already."

* * *

Chloe floated in the pool behind Carmen's house, resting after doing her laps and thinking about Zack. She really liked him, but she dreaded what she'd have to tell him if their feelings kept growing. She had flowers on her coffee table with a card that said, "The courtship begins?"

She hadn't been serious when she'd kidded about courtship and flowers. He had to know that. Maybe he and Bonnie had shopped for the flowers. Bonnie would have loved that, and Zack would have had a good time making his mom happy.

Chloe had called to thank Zack for the flowers, but she'd had to leave a message. Maybe he and Bonnie had gone to Vegas without her. Good for them. And good for her sisters for having dinner plans tonight. As for herself, she would have the single woman's dinner of choice—a bag of microwaved popcorn.

Lunch in Solvang with Bonnie and Zack was at a charming Danish inn. Like other tourists, they wore casual clothes on this warm April day. Chloe had worn layered tank tops, jean capri pants and flip-flops. Bonnie looked adorable in her dainty lavender top, white pants and walking shoes. And Zack… The man had women turning their heads.

Chloe understood. She could hardly keep her eyes off him herself. Tall, lean, well-built, wearing a blue T-shirt and white shorts, the guy stood out in a crowd.

Solvang's business section was a tree-shaded street with old country architecture that made Chloe feel as if she were in a Copenhagen neighborhood. Groups of ladies had come to have lunch and shop. Sweethearts, old and young, strolled hand in hand, concentrating more on each other than their surroundings.

Chloe wished she were half of a pair, confident in the love of a man by her side. Well, not just any man, but the one meandering in and out of the stores with Bonnie.

In a darling little bookstore, Zack looked over her shoulder while she turned the pages of a Hans Christian Andersen book. She barely noticed the book. It took all of her concentration to deal with her wobbly legs, a condition brought on by feeling Zack's breath on her neck. That was what she got for wearing her hair in a ponytail today.

She'd have to wear it that way more often.

"Kids," Bonnie said, coming up to them, "you are being so sweet to me, but I'm sorry. This isn't working out."

Chloe dropped the book. Zack just stared.

"The problem is I'm a power shopper. I want a glimpse inside every store in Solvang, but we're moving so slowly, we'd need to stay all night and shop tomorrow."

Chloe bit her lip to hold back a smile. Bonnie was about to disappear again.

"Is that what you want, Mom?" Zack looked concerned. "You want to stay overnight?"

"No, I just want to shop on my own, see it all and have dinner in Santa Barbara like we planned."

Points to Bonnie for coming up with a matchmaker move that sounded logical, even to Chloe. She looked at Zack, sure that he recognized her intention, but he didn't seem to.

"We'll speed up, Mom. You set the pace. Chloe and

I will watch for when you're ready to move on and stick with you like glue."

"That's sweet, Zack, but I really would like to be on my own. Why don't you two rent one of those tandem bikes and see more of the town."

"I think we should stick together," Zack said firmly.

As if he'd never spoken, Bonnie said, "I'll meet you back at that chocolate shop in about—" She checked her watch. "Three hours. That ought to do it."

"Three hours! Mom, won't that wear you out?"

"Zack, in a place like this I could shop all day! There's nothing like it back home. The windmills…the cobblestone streets!" Bonnie's face took on a dreamy expression. "If I could just be on my own for a while…I'll feel like I'm back in Denmark…with Grandma Jorgensen."

Chloe got busy, putting her book back on the shelf. Bonnie deserved an Oscar. The "Grandma Jorgensen" thing? Wonderful!

She risked a glance at Zack and really struggled not to laugh. His tender expression was perfect, as if he thought his mother intended to commune with Grandma Jorgensen.

Bonnie reached up and patted his face and was out of the store before the doorbells stopped jingling.

"I guess we're on our own," Zack said, looking around the store, his hands on his hips like a guy who had a job to tackle and didn't know where to begin.

"The car's not parked far away," he said. "We could drive to the place where they rent the tandem bikes."

"It *would* be the California way—driving to a place we can exercise."

He smiled at her little joke. "I guess we could jog there."

"Jog?" Chloe looked pointedly at her flip-flops. "Would you settle for a fast walk?"

He flashed his heart-stealing smile. "I'd settle for anything that didn't involve shopping." He opened the door, setting off the bells again, and gestured for her to precede him. They were barely through the door when he put his hand on the small of her back, as if to guide her.

It was just a courtesy, but the light touch gave her a genuine girlfriend feeling. If he wanted to leave his hand there for the next three hours, she'd be okay with that.

But she was being selfish. "You know, Zack, if you'd like to catch up with your mother and take that virtual tour with Grandma Jorgensen, I can rent a bike for one, or I can hang out in that chocolate shop for three hours."

He burst out laughing. "In all these years, I've heard next to nothing about my Danish ancestors. Mom's never been to Denmark. She pulled Grandma Jorgensen out of thin air."

"You knew? I thought you were being such a sweet, sympathetic son."

"I was! I am! After spending time with her yesterday, I've got it. She's worried that I'm too shy to find a wife."

"You! Beverly Hills' most eligible bachelor?"

"I *was* shy before I left home. It's giving her such pleasure to think she's helping me. Do you mind letting her think she is?"

Chloe was all for making Bonnie happy, but no one

liked to be lied to. "And when she's back home and asks for an update, what are you going to tell her?"

"I think that depends on you." His blue eyes locked with hers. "Will you want to see me after Mom goes home?"

"Are you saying, *you'll* want to see *me?*" Her knees could buckle any minute.

"Very much, though if you're involved with someone…"

"I'm not." It was flattering that he'd think she might be.

"Chloe, I know we've only known each other a few days, but I don't want us to stop seeing each other when Mom goes home."

She didn't either, but she had to ask, "And this has nothing to do with making your mother happy?"

He broke pace and faced her. "Mom's little maneuvers have allowed us time to get to know each other more quickly than we might have otherwise, but that's it. Are we clear on that?"

This was a new side to Zack. Maybe that worked for him at the hospital, but she thought it was funny. She tried not to giggle, but the giggle wouldn't stay put.

"I like the giggle, by the way," he said, relaxing.

That was good because another one escaped.

He laughed and reached for her hand. "We're going to have fun, Chloe Kilgannon."

They were holding hands like a couple—two people who belonged to each other! It took her breath, but who needed to breathe? She'd done that all of her life.

"Let's see, tomorrow you leave for Denver, and I'm taking Mom to the San Diego Zoo. Saturday and

Sunday morning, you'll be at your conference. So, the next time I'll see you will be at your parents' house for Sunday-night supper?"

That was three days away—and already she missed him. Would she wake up at some point and realize this had only been a dream?

"Mom leaves Monday morning, but that's still a vacation day for me. Can we get together after you get off work?"

"If you want to," she said tentatively. She still struggled to believe he'd want to see her when Bonnie wasn't around.

He gave her his stern look again. "If I *want* to? Chloe, are we on the same page or not? Yes, I want to see you—Monday, Tuesday, maybe every day."

She was in way over her head. "Zack, I've been out of the country a long time, so I've got to ask…when you say you want to 'see me,' are you talking about a date?"

He smiled. "Yeah, I am."

"Okay. Then, when you talk about a date, are you talking about exclusivity or will you be dating other women, too?"

"No, just you."

She swallowed hard. "So are you saying you want me to be your girlfriend? Or is it called something else these days?"

"I don't know, but girlfriend? That's good."

Catching a good breath should not be this difficult. *Go for the joke. That was the way to survive.* "I usually know a guy a full week before I agree to be his girlfriend, but you are a good-lookin' guy, and you've got a nice mom."

His face broke into a full-out grin. "Thanks. Are there some rules or guidelines we should know? Like, if I forget that it's our anniversary a month from now, you won't be angry?"

"You're planning to be my boyfriend that long?"

He did a step back and clutched his chest. "I'm pretty sure a girlfriend doesn't distrust her boyfriend from the get-go."

"Well, I'm new at this. About Monday—I'd love to do something with you."

He pulled her down to sit on a tree-shaded bench. "What would you like to do?" He looked at her as if the world were hers for the asking.

She wasn't in the habit of thinking that big. "What would *you* like?"

"I kind of like what we're doing now."

"Sightseeing?"

"Holding hands. It's nice."

It was spectacular!

"If Mom could see us now, can you imagine her reaction?"

"We're holding hands for Bonnie's sake?" she yelped, trying to pull her hand away. He held it tighter.

"Chloe," he said, his voice rising in warning. "Don't go there. Not even to make Mom happy would I use her as an excuse."

"I don't see you as a man who needs an excuse."

His mouth lifted in a surprisingly uncertain smile. "The things that impress other women I've met don't impress you."

"You impress me, or we wouldn't be holding hands."

"You're not impressed with what I do for a living, or social status or the material things I could provide."

That was all true.

"You're strong, Chloe. You have goals you wouldn't give up."

She shook her head. "No, I have *values* I wouldn't give up. I try to sense God's will and be ready for change."

"But you'd never give up your love of children."

"No, I wouldn't. Loving children is as much a part of me as surgery is of you, but I *would* give up the idea of having children of my own. In fact, I'd like to adopt."

"Really?"

She felt a twinge of guilt at the lie. She hadn't *given* up anything. It had been taken from her. It was wrong to shade the truth, but she wasn't ready to reveal her darkest secret to a man she'd known all of six days, boyfriend or not.

If they were together a month from now, that would be soon enough to tell him. "How do you feel about adopting?" she asked.

"After your workshop presentation, I thought about it, though I hadn't thought much about children before then."

He was nervous about her reaction. That was plain to see.

"We can talk about serious stuff another time. I believe you said we were going to have fun."

His relieved smile touched her heart. "I did say that, didn't I? Ready to pedal through town on a bike?"

Holding Zack's hand, she felt ready to pedal all the way back to L.A.

Chapter Eleven

Zack lay in his bed, watching the sunlight play on the ceiling, wondering what Chloe was doing this morning in Denver. After their day in Solvang and their evening in Santa Barbara, his feelings for her had rocketed so fast that he hadn't planned to talk to her until tomorrow night when she got home.

But he'd gone online, surfed for the Love Into Action conferences and discovered the hotel where she'd be staying. His flowers had been waiting for her when she checked in. This time the card read, "Still my girlfriend?"

He'd missed her thank-you call. But she'd left a message that he'd played many times just to hear the smile in her voice.

Was she nervous about her workshop today? Was she wearing the blue suit she'd worn a week ago? He hadn't been the same since that day.

He rolled over on his stomach. Thinking about Chloe had taken over his life. Yesterday he'd taken Mom to the San Diego Zoo, and he'd thought about Chloe getting ready for her trip. At SeaWorld, he'd thought of her checking into the airport and he'd even wondered about the person sitting beside her on the plane.

Had it been a sweet-faced grandmother or some handsome businessman who had asked her to dinner? Had she told him she was seeing someone?

If he could get this upset over a guy who might not exist, that had to be jealousy talking. It was a first for him, and it was one ugly emotion.

But he'd never met anyone like Chloe. She had this amazing knack for finding the positive side of everyone and everything. It was reassuring to know she would likely find his redeeming qualities on the days he might mess up.

And she was so pretty, though she didn't seem to realize it. Her long dark hair was beautiful, and her chocolate-brown eyes just drew him in. What would it be like to hold her in his arms?

"Zack?" his mom called with a happy lilt from the other side of his bedroom door. "I have your breakfast."

"Come on in, Mom."

She came through the door carrying a tray of steaming hot coffee, fresh orange juice and an omelet. "I thought you might enjoy a little pampering."

"Breakfast in bed?" he said with a smile, sitting up and throwing a pillow behind his back. The extra coffee mug on the tray must be for her.

"We've been on the go every day," she said. "I thought it might be nice if we just stayed around the condo and rested." She arranged a pillow on the other side of his king-size bed and got comfortable before taking that extra mug.

"What time shall we leave to see my office?" he

asked. Somehow it was Saturday and Mom still hadn't seen Brennan Medical Clinic, the one place he'd wanted to show off.

"How about tomorrow?" she said charmingly. "Let's just be lazy today."

On Sunday, the place would be lifeless. Even today, there wouldn't be much activity. "I thought you wanted to see the Crystal Cathedral tomorrow and have fried chicken at Knott's Berry Farm. If we do that and add a tour of my office, we won't make it to the Kilgannons' on time. What would you like to cut out?"

She lost her sweet smile and looked disappointed. "Nothing. I guess I can have a lazy day when I get home. We'd better see your office today."

He wished she didn't sound so resigned. "It's too bad that you won't get to meet the Brennans. They're never in on Saturday."

"I've met Collin and Albert Brennan."

"Yes, but you haven't met Collin's father or his uncle James. I really wanted you to meet J. T. Brennan, patriarch of the Brennan dynasty."

"Will any of them be at the Kilgannons' tomorrow night?"

"They might be. They're part of the group that has a standing invitation."

"It will be my last night here," she said softly, as if to herself. Brightening, she added, "We'd better make the most of the time. I'll be ready before you are!"

He drank the juice and set the tray aside before heading to the shower. He'd loved having Mom here, but he would be so glad to get back to his normal routine.

Breakfast in bed would not be on his agenda. He'd never really cared for it, but even as a kid he'd understood it was her way to show him love. He could still hear Dad's angry protest that Mom shouldn't be waiting on "the kid."

Most of the time he didn't think back on those days—too many memories, too much pain. He should take a page from Chloe's book and try to find something positive about his dad. He thought about it while he showered and dressed.

The only positive thing he came up with was that he'd never have to deal with his father again.

It was noon by the time Zack drove into the Brennan Medical Clinic parking lot. "Dr. Z. Hemingway!" his mother read, noting his parking space. "Very impressive, Zack. You've worked very hard for this."

"I have, but I owe a lot to Albert Brennan. I don't think I would be part of such a prestigious group as Brennan Medical if I hadn't met him that day at Stanford. The only BMC doctors who are as young as me are the founder's grandkids."

"Yes…well…the clinic is certainly an impressive building." She got out of the car and studied the building. "I've always loved Spanish architecture—the tiled roof, the pale yellow stucco, the arched windows. It pleases the eye."

There were few cars in the parking lot, and the lobby was as lifeless as he'd expected. He showed her around the orthopedic wing, including the suite he shared with Albert and several others—each with their own sub-specialties. Mom complimented the upscale decor, but her face crumbled when he pointed out the picture on his office credenza.

She picked it up. "Of all our family pictures, this is the one you chose?"

He swallowed hard around the lump in his throat and could only nod. In the picture she was young and beautiful, and she was kissing the little boy in her arms. When he looked at that picture, he remembered what it felt like to be loved.

"I'm so glad I saw this," she said, wiping tears away.

"There's something else you're going to like."

He took her hand and, without people to greet, it didn't take long to reach the wall of framed photographs, three rows deep, that he wanted her to see. He stopped in the middle where there was a special grouping of pictures.

"All of the doctors with offices at the clinic have pictures here, but the doctors in this center grouping are the Brennans. Top row, center—that's J. T. Brennan Sr., founder of the clinic. Underneath his picture are his three sons, all doctors with offices here, and beneath them are *their* children with offices here. Look who's on that row!"

He'd been waiting for this moment. Having his photo two down from the founder's meant more to him than every material possession he had.

"Zack! What's your picture doing there?" Her eyes widened, and her face lost color, just like before.

He took her arm. "Mom, what's the matter?"

"I'm fine," she said, sounding like it even if she didn't look it. "Why are you with the Brennans, Zack?"

"I'm an honorary Brennan. You heard Albert Brennan say that he and his wife claimed me as their own since they don't have children. He asked if I minded having my picture in the grouping since his two brothers each had a child there. Everyone around here knows that Albert took me under his wing. The clinic grapevine spreads news faster than CNN."

His mother clung to his arm and stared at the pictures as if she didn't quite understand. He'd expected her to be happy, but she looked as if she might cry again.

"Everyone refers to J. T. Brennan as 'the chief,'" Zack said, pointing to the founder's picture. "It's a title he earned as the hospital chief of staff at Cedar Hills. Dr. Brennan's nearly ninety, but he still comes in every day."

"He's not still seeing patients?" she asked.

"No, but he's the heart and soul of the clinic and sets the tone around here. The rumor is he's hanging on because his three sons don't want to replace him as CEO, and neither do his grandchildren. Well, one of the grandchildren might, but he's not a stable guy."

Zack pointed to the picture of the chief's eldest son. "James has three children who are doctors, though only one has an office here. That's Beth, who's a pediatrician." He pointed to her picture. "Mom, you'll be happy to know that I once thought about dating her."

"Albert's niece?" Her eyes went wide.

"I struck out, Mom," he said with a grin. "Beth fell

in love with her office nurse—a great guy—and married him."

She turned back to the wall of photographs and pointed to the third of the chief's sons. "And this is—"

"Charles," Zack said, "though everyone calls him—"

"Charlie," Mom said softly.

"You're right. He looks like a Charlie, doesn't he? Albert is never Al, and James is never Jim, but Charlie's always Charlie, a guy with an eye for the ladies."

"That's his reputation?"

"It's more than a reputation. He's an embarrassment to the family."

"Is he married?"

"He's had a couple of wives, but he's single now. You met his son, Collin, at the Hilltop."

"Does Collin have brothers or sisters?"

"No, he's an only child like me."

"Is Collin close to his parents?"

"With his mother. She raised him."

"Here you are!"

Zack turned at the familiar voice and his mouth dropped open. The chief limped toward them, leaning heavily on his cane.

"Zack, I heard your mother was in the building, and I didn't want her to get away without meeting her myself."

How had the chief heard about it? The only person they'd seen had been the security guard in his office off the lobby.

Though it was Saturday, the snowy-haired patriarch was dressed as if it were a regular workday, and he looked very sharp in a navy double-breasted blazer and white dress pants. His age-worn face was wreathed in a smile.

Zack made the introductions properly as his mother had taught him to do, and she extended her hand. "How do you do, Doctor," she said with a chilly smile that was borderline rude. Where was her charm, her charisma?

"I see that you're looking at pictures of the family," the chief said proudly.

"Yes. I was surprised to see my son included."

Ignoring the challenge in her tone, the chief said, "Ah, yes. That was my son's doing. Albert and Amy have no children, and Zack means a lot to them, as he does to all of us. I hope you don't mind?"

"Mind? Of course not. Every mother wants her son to find favor."

Zack knew when his mother was sincere and when she was only pretending to be. Without a doubt, she'd taken an instant dislike to the chief. But why? Everyone loved this good man.

Zack's dismay must have shown on his face because she added more cordially, "I can only imagine how proud you must be to have your children and grandchildren working with you in this marvelous clinic."

"Having my family work with me was a young man's dream. It's been an old man's joy." The chief's voice quavered a bit, revealing his age. "Mrs. Hemingway, why don't you and I get better acquainted in my office? I want to sing your son's praises, but he doesn't need to get a big head hearing them."

"That's what his father always said."

Zack's head seemed to spin. She was still accepting Dad's excuse for being so hurtful?

"Excuse us, Zack," the chief said. "Make yourself busy while we chat."

"How busy, Chief? Five minutes…ten…more?"

"I expect we'll visit long enough for you to do some work in your office. Why don't I call you there when we're through?"

Zack nodded and sent his mother an encouraging smile. She raised one challenging brow. He smiled to himself, getting the message. Mom didn't need encouragement to face the unknown when it was only a chat with one elderly man, no matter how important he was.

Zack watched the pair until they turned the corner. What did Dr. Brennan have to say to Mom that would take so much time?

As long as he had some time to kill, why not call Chloe? It was almost 1:00 p.m. here, so it would be 2:00 p.m. in Denver. She would probably be in a workshop, but he could leave a message.

As expected, he got her voice mail, and he said, "Hi Chloe! I was just wondering how your morning workshop went. Call me when you can…if you have time…if you want to…" How could he end this? "Nice talking to you."

He closed his eyes, smacked the phone against his forehead and wished he'd never called. He had the dating confidence of a six-year-old, but did Chloe have to know it?

His cell phone rang and the caller ID showed it was Chloe. "Hey there!" he said, lowering his voice, trying to make up for sounding so silly before.

"Hi!" she said breathlessly.

He heard the smile in her voice and relaxed. He didn't have to be someone he wasn't with Chloe.

"I had my phone on vibrate and couldn't answer until I left a meeting. I'm so glad you called."

He swung his feet up on his desk and leaned back in his chair, imagining her eyes, her smile, her face. "How's it going?"

"I was just as nervous as last week, but I got over it. I guess I'm doing okay, but I'd rather be riding a tandem bike in Solvang with you."

"Sure, you would. You coasted while I did all the pedaling."

"Did not! Not all the time."

The lighthearted banter was just what he needed. "Have you met any cute guys in Denver?"

"No, but there was this one guy on the plane—"

"Tell me he didn't ask you out."

"Ask me out?" She giggled. "No, but I held him most of the way."

Adrenaline shot through him like an arrow to the target.

"His mom was flying with three little guys under the age of five. I got to take care of the nine-month-old baby."

Zack sagged in his chair, feeling relieved...and stupid.

"Do you like babies, Zack?"

She wanted him to say he did. He would lose points if he didn't. "I honestly don't know," he said, sidestepping. "The babies I've known have mostly been sedated."

"And you're an only child, so there are no nieces and nephews."

"Not a one. But I've been working on your suggestion that we become more aware of the little kids in our lives."

"Really?" She sounded as pleased as he'd hoped.

It might be a first for him, caring enough about a woman to talk about kids. "When Mom and I were at the zoo yesterday, I had a better time watching the little kids than the animals. I kept one little girl from taking a nasty fall. I'd give more examples, but I don't like to brag."

"You can brag all you want. I'm proud of you!"

Simple words, but they made him ridiculously happy. "Anything we do for children is better than nothing at all, right?"

"That is so right! You're such a quick learner."

"Chloe?"

"Yes, I'm here."

He wished she were closer. "I miss you."

There was such a pause after his words that he wondered if they'd been disconnected. "Chloe?" he said tentatively, to see if she was still there.

"I'm here." He heard her take a deep breath. "I have this problem. I can't think what to say when people touch my heart."

That could be a problem because he had the same affliction. "When am I going to see you?"

"Aren't you going to be at my parents' house Sunday night?"

"Mom and I will be there, but I'm asking when can I see *you,* just you."

"Like, for a 'welcome home' hug?"

"To start with."

Again she paused so long he wondered about a disconnect, but then she said, "As soon as I get there, and I can't wait to get home."

Chapter Twelve

It was the first time Chloe had been home in two years, but she had no expectation that her parents would roll out the red carpet, especially since she'd skipped Sunday night supper again last week. She hadn't found the courage, but tonight she was determined that nothing her parents could say or do would upset her. At twenty-eight, she'd learned the value in turning the other cheek, and she'd left their meeting in God's hands.

As she walked toward the house, she saw her father and Albert Brennan admiring an antique sports car that was probably her dad's latest toy. She didn't begrudge him the pleasure of having something he wanted, but she couldn't help thinking how many people in a third-world country could survive on the price of that toy.

They looked up and her dad said, "You're late."

"It's nice to see you, too, Dad." The edge of sarcasm in her voice wasn't in sync with her prayers for reconciliation. She had to do better. Risking rejection, she went right up to him and put both arms around his neck as she'd seen her sisters do.

He gave her a perfunctory pat on the back and pulled away, but Albert reached out to claim a real hug.

He whispered in her ear, "There's a young man who's been pacing this drive for the last hour."

That was what she wanted to hear. She walked toward the pool area where the guests would be and saw Zack crossing the lawn, holding drinks in both hands apparently intended for his mom and Albert's wife sitting under a shady tree. He wore dress pants in a darker shade of cream than his shirt and looked wonderful.

"Chloe!" Zack stopped in mid stride. The gladness in his face was all she could have hoped for. If she followed her impulse, she would run to him and hope he would catch her in his arms, but she'd already taken her risk of the day with Dad.

Walking slowly toward Zack, he walked just as slowly toward her and their eyes locked as if they were alone.

"Give me those drinks," Cate said, scooping them out of Zack's hands.

"Chloe's here," he murmured.

"I can see that," Cate said with a soft laugh. "Chloe, why don't you take Zack to Mom's gardening room."

"Thanks, Cate," Chloe murmured. That was the one probable place they could be alone.

Zack held out his arms with a welcoming smile that made Chloe's heart leap. What was better than knowing where she belonged?

"Where's the gardening room?" he said, his voice low, just for her. "I can't wait…to hear about your trip."

Judging by the way he was looking at her, he wasn't interested in traveling details. "We'll need to cut through the library," she said, opening a side door and leading the way.

They'd barely gotten inside the house when he stopped, cupped her head and said, "I've missed you." With his eyes on her mouth, he lowered his head until his lips touched hers softly just for a moment.

"Hey, you two!" Cate whispered. "People are coming. Get a move on unless you're through with the welcome-home ritual."

"Where's that gardening room?" Zack murmured.

"Here you are!" Bonnie had found them. "Chloe, we missed you!"

The feeling was mutual, even if Chloe did regret Bonnie's timing. Zack put a few inches between them, but he still held her hand. She gave Bonnie a one-arm hug and asked about her San Diego trip and her tour of Brennan Medical Clinic.

Bonnie didn't seem to notice that Zack had steered them outside to join the guests by the pool, she was so busy telling about her San Diego trip. She didn't mention the clinic or seeing Zack's picture with the Brennans. From Carmen, Chloe knew that Zack had looked forward to surprising his mother with that. Had Bonnie not realized how fortunate Zack was to have a mentor like Albert Brennan?

Speaking of the Brennans, Albert and Amy seemed to be the only Brennans present. Usually there were others.

"Chloe!" Her mother shrieked as if she had just spotted her.

She hadn't. Chloe had been watching her mother from the corner of her eye since they'd joined the group at the pool, and her mother had been watching them. If she considered this the moment to maximize on a big welcome, Chloe wouldn't question the delay. She just prayed it was real.

Before her mother reached her, Carmen and Cate closed ranks on one side of her. On the other side Zack tightened his grip on her hand, and Bonnie took his other arm. This might be overkill in the support department, but Ava Kilgannon *was* known for her unpredictability.

"Look, everyone!" Ava's voice rose to address her guests. "It's our prodigal daughter! Chloe has come home!"

As an embarrassing moment, it barely ranked a three on a five-point scale. Chloe had expected much worse.

"But look quickly," her mother added, walking toward them, a petite Latin beauty in a tangerine-colored pants outfit and very high heels. "Our Chloe has a habit of disappearing. She's here today and gone tomorrow."

It may have been like that in the past, but had her mother forgotten the illness that had brought her home to stay?

"Don't get too attached to our Chloe," her mother went on, tossing her dark hair like a young girl. "You never know when she'll show up again."

Carmen groaned. "Do something, Cate. Save Mom from herself."

"When Mom's on a roll, an earthquake wouldn't change her course," Cate muttered.

When her mother stopped in front of Chloe, she eyed her from top to bottom. "I can't believe this tall girl is my daughter? Unless you bend down, Chloe, I can't even give you a hug."

Chloe bent for the hug, glad to have an excuse to hide her face.

"Your beautiful daughter was the star of a conference workshop I attended recently," Bonnie spoke up loyally. "She kept a large audience spellbound with her experiences and her gift for speaking. Ava, your daughter is a woman any mother would be proud to call her own."

Good for Bonnie! Chloe beamed at her.

"I'm proud of all my daughters," her mother said, jutting one hip. She played with her trendy necklace and flashed a megawatt smile. "They are all exceptional, and I am just their mother."

Chloe exchanged a look with Carmen. Nothing had changed. The world still revolved around Mom.

"Ava, I want to thank you," Zack said.

"Darling, Zack, whatever for?" Ava Kilgannon extended one hand toward Cate and the other to Zack as if they were a couple. "You're practically family."

"I appreciate that," Zack said. "You and Sterling have been very good to me. Carmen and Cate are great friends. And now that I've gotten to know Chloe, I've—"

"Discovered that we saved the best for last," Carmen inserted generously.

"Discovered that Chloe's the perfect height for Zack!" Cate added with a grin.

Their mother snapped her fingers. "Girls! Don't be silly."

Zack put his arm around Chloe's waist as if he were claiming her and looked at the top of Chloe's head. "I hadn't thought about it before you mentioned it, Cate, but you're right. Chloe's perfect for me."

Aghast, Ava protested, "She didn't say—"

"They do make a nice-looking couple," Bonnie interrupted as if on cue.

Ava glared at Bonnie, and it looked as if a cutting remark were on its way.

Zack may have seen it, too, because he said quickly, "Mom and Chloe have become very good friends this week."

Ava looked startled.

"You have met my mother, haven't you, Ava?"

Chloe could see recognition dawn and, with it, a major attitude change.

With great charm, her mother said, "I believe we met when you arrived, Mrs. Hemingway, but we have yet to become acquainted. Perhaps you will sit beside me at dinner?"

"It's just Bonnie, and I would be happy to."

"Good. If you'll excuse me, I'll check on our dinner." Without another look at her daughters or Zack, Ava hurried toward the house.

Chloe felt herself sag in relief, but Zack was there, his arm around her.

"I think that went as well as we could have expected," Carmen said as if she were describing the end of a surgery.

Cate tucked her long blond hair behind one ear and let out a pent-up breath. "Bonnie, you have no idea how bad that could have been. Our mother is a true drama queen, and when she gets an idea into her head, she doesn't rest until she gets her way."

"I'm not sure I understand," Bonnie said, and her blue eyes did look confused.

Cate tried to explain. "Mom has it in her mind that Zack is *my* guy. No offense intended, but he's *not*."

"And you'll probably see our father shove Zack *my* way before the night is over," Carmen added dryly. "Bonnie, your son is our very good friend, but Cate and I prefer to find our own men."

Bonnie's blue eyes held remorse. "Of course you do. I'm afraid I'm just as guilty of pushing Zack toward marriage, and I do love Chloe. You poor kids with your meddling mothers."

"Don't feel bad on my account," Chloe said. "I was flattered."

"You were?" Zack said, amazement in his eyes. "I thought you were just being a good sport."

"Well, that, too." A giggle escaped.

"I love that giggle," he said to her sisters.

Cate threw up her hands. "It must be true love. Nobody likes that giggle."

The dinner gong sounded and Bonnie looked around, startled.

"Dinner's ready," Carmen said, taking Bonnie's arm.

"I've never known a family with a dinner gong," Bonnie said. "I'm so impressed."

"Well, good," Cate said ruefully. "At this house it's all about making an impression."

"I know that Carmen is a surgeon, but what is it you do, Cate?" Bonnie asked.

"I'm a fitness trainer. I design fitness programs for clients and supervise their progress. Zack's my client, but I don't charge him since he's practically family."

"And Cate gets free knee surgeries as needed," Zack added.

The teasing continued as they found their seats—Bonnie at a huge oval table beside Ava; the three sisters and Zack at a quartet table they dubbed the kids' table. There were other side tables for guests and a beautiful buffet set with colorful salads, a big bowl of chilled shrimp on ice, and an assortment of meat and vegetables hot off the grill.

Chloe had dreaded this first time back in her parents' home, but sitting here with her sisters and Zack, she had to wonder why she'd been so concerned about coming back home.

As the guests finished their meal, they pushed back from their tables and turned their attention to their host. For a man of his age, Chloe's father was blessed by a full head of silver hair, a handsome, barely lined face and just a bit of a paunch under his taupe shirt and pants. Relaxed, in a good mood, he stood at the head of the big table, one hand in his pants pocket, the other holding a glass of sparkling water.

"So, Dad still does his stand-up comic thing?" Chloe asked.

"Why else would he host these Sunday-night suppers?" Cate asked dryly.

"He's pretty good at it, though," Carmen defended. "And he did just provide an excellent meal and the opportunity for our friends to relax and enjoy each other's company."

No one would argue with that, but Chloe had wondered why he hated her clowning when he himself loved to entertain. Some men might have called her a chip off the old block and been proud.

Tapping on a glass for attention, he began. "Tonight we welcome Zack Hemingway's mother from Illinois, Bonnie."

During the applause, Zack zipped out of his chair and gave Bonnie a hug.

Their father gestured to their table and said, "And we have with us our world-traveling daughter, Chloe!"

The group turned her way to applaud. A murmur of appreciation went through the room.

Chloe had known most of these people her entire life. They'd been present on other Sunday nights like this one to applaud when she'd graduated from college as a teenager and when she'd received her master's not long after that. And she'd been there for them, clowning at their children's parties and sending their children letters from abroad. It was her community, and she was glad to be part of it again.

Zack bent and said softly, "Welcome home, Chloe!"

It was one of the best moments she'd ever known.

"It seems that Chloe is here to stay for a while," her father said with a jovial smile. "Most of you have shelled out big money for your kids' education, so you'll understand how justifiably proud I am to announce that Chloe's taken a job that actually pays!"

There was a smatter of applause and a murmur of

good-natured congratulations. Chloe pretended she was fine with it all.

"Yes, Chloe's finally self-supporting, and she's only twenty-eight!"

That stung. Time and again, her parents had claimed their financial support was their way to participate in the work she did for children. Her pride wouldn't have allowed her to take their money to live on if they hadn't been very convincing about wanting to do it.

But now her father made it sound as if she'd been a burden. Was that the way he truly felt or was this part of his routine? Was she reading too much into his comments or had she been blind?

"Our deal with Chloe," her father continued, "was that her travels would provide research opportunities. By this time, I thought we'd have another doctor in the family, even if it was only a doctor of philosophy."

He made it sound like good-natured ribbing, and that was how Chloe tried to take it.

"Of course, her mother and I are still waiting for the dissertation she said she would write…and we paid for."

Zack felt sick to his stomach. Sterling knew how to tell a story and keep a crowd entertained. Going for the laugh at someone's expense wasn't unusual for comics, but a man making fun of his daughter hit below the belt.

"Ava and I tried to raise daughters who would *do* what they *said* they would do, but our Chloe does it *her* way. She's our little rebel."

"Not so little," Ava added.

That got a laugh, too, but not from Zack. If this public scolding, disguised as humor, was what Chloe experienced when she came home, was it any wonder she left and seldom came back?

He wanted to get her and his mom out of here now. Could he do it without making a scene? Sterling wouldn't forgive him for that, and he could make Zack's life rough. As chief of surgery, Sterling had recommended Zack for Madison Haines's operation. Just as easily, Sterling could stop recommending him. It wouldn't matter how good Zack was at his job.

Lord, how can I end this?

"Sterling!" he called out, not sure where he was heading.

"Yes, Zack. I see you're surrounded by Kilgannon women."

"I am indeed, and it's my pleasure." The crowded tittered.

"As well it ought to be," Sterling joked.

"It just occurred to me that you and Ava are to be congratulated for the support you gave to Chloe." He stepped behind Chloe's chair. That gave him a perfect vantage to speak to Sterling and his guests without getting sidetracked by Chloe's expressive eyes. His feelings for her were so deep at the moment, he could barely concentrate on the task at hand.

"We don't expect recognition for educating our daughters," Sterling said, "and we treated them all the same. We paid for Carmen's education as a surgeon, and for Cate to become a fitness trainer—although that didn't touch the wallet much. Naturally, we would pay for Chloe to gather data for her dissertation. We just didn't expect it to drag out for eight years."

"Every doctor in this room knows what it's like to choose between taking the time to publish or make sick people well," Zack said. "Chloe hasn't stopped to write the paper because she's been busy living a superlative life."

There was a murmur of agreement among the guests.

"I was with my mother last week when Chloe got a standing ovation for her work with children who'd lost everything—their families, their homes, everything that was dear to them. I've asked myself, could I have done what she's done? I know I couldn't, but she realized somebody had to care for little children who couldn't care for themselves. She stepped up. Congratulations, Ava and Sterling. You raised Chloe well."

Chairs scraped against the marble floor as the guests rose and applauded. Zack looked down at Chloe. Would this validation make up for the sting of her dad's remarks?

She looked at him in awe. Had no one ever stood up for her before? Albert and Amy came over and gave Chloe a hug, and others followed until Sterling tapped a spoon against a water glass to get their attention again.

When the guests were back in their seats, Sterling said, "Thank you for that impassioned speech, Zack. I know how much you abhor public speaking, so that makes it all the more meaningful."

Zack would have preferred to hear good words about Chloe.

"Well, Chloe, what can I say?" Her dad strolled to their table and stood in front of her.

She looked up at her father with hope in her beautiful eyes. Zack's chest felt so heavy, he could barely breathe. Sterling had to treat Chloe well. He just had to.

"So, now, you're home to stay," Sterling began, "and you've done us proud, even without keeping your word."

"But I always keep my word," she said quickly.

She stood abruptly and faced her father, her shoulders back and her chin high. She wasn't as tall as he was, but anyone could see where she'd gotten her height. Where she'd gotten her dignity was anybody's guess.

"Dad's right." She spoke to the room. "I did begin my work with Love Into Action to gather research data. I just didn't realize the plan we made when I was a teenager was still in effect. Like Zack said, when it became a choice between writing a paper and responding to the need I saw...well, there just wasn't any choice. I thought I had Dad's blessing. His checks for my support kept coming in. Wasn't that great?" She led the applause.

Zack would have stood beside her, but she was doing fine, facing her dad down, on her own.

"It's been great to see you all," she said, picking up her purse, "but it seems I have a debt to pay. If you'll excuse me, I'll get right on it."

She was out of the room before Zack could respond.

"I don't think I'll hold my breath, waiting for that dissertation," Sterling joked, addressing his guests, all old friends or colleagues.

They didn't smile back. Sterling had crossed the line.

"How's she going to write a dissertation without research data?" he asked as if to prove a point.

"She has her research data," Carmen said, standing. "She's mailed it to me regularly for eight years."

Cate stood beside Carmen and glared at her dad. "Chloe'll have that dissertation knocked out before you get your big foot out of your mouth, Dad."

"Cate!" Ava called out in reprimand.

"Sorry, Mom, but you know it's true." Cate linked her arm in Carmen's and followed Chloe.

All the guests were rising to their feet, and the evening was clearly over.

"No need to rush off," Sterling said.

"Ready to leave, Mom?" Zack asked. It wasn't really a question.

"More than ready," she said for his ears only.

Chapter Thirteen

In the car, Zack drove without speaking. Would Sterling blame that awful scene on Chloe? What happened now? A mean streak in a powerful man could be hard to escape.

"I'm sorry everything ended so badly," Mom said, breaking the silence.

"*I'm* sorry that the one time you were a guest of the Kilgannons, it was so uncomfortable, Mom. For the record, I've never seen Sterling like that."

She was silent so long, Zack glanced at his mother. Tears were running down her cheeks.

"Mom?" What was wrong? Quickly, he replayed what he'd just said and came up with nothing.

"I'm just feeling bad for Chloe." She fished tissues from her purse and patted the tears away. "The thing that gets you is the surprise element of unkindness. You never know when people will be less than their best."

That was one way to say it.

"But wasn't Chloe wonderful? She had to have been angry, but she didn't return ugly words with more of the same. That young woman lives her faith!"

She really did. Zack wasn't up to her standard, but he thought he'd like to be. Hadn't Carmen made some comment about Chloe's faith rubbing off on her? Apparently it was happening to him, too.

His cell phone rang. The ID said it was Carmen.

"Zack, we're on our way home. We didn't get a chance to tell your mother goodbye, and I know she flies out tomorrow. Would you mind stopping by for a while?"

He'd planned to stop by even without an invitation, and he hadn't been thinking about Mom. He'd just wanted to be with Chloe.

Carmen was waiting at the door when they arrived. "Thank you for coming," she said, hugging them both, as if this were a funeral gathering.

Maybe it was. Zack felt as if someone had died.

"Cate and Chloe are on the lanai," Carmen said. "Shall we join them?"

For once, Zack didn't feel like being a gentleman. Instead of letting the women precede him, he stepped around and took long strides to the lanai. He was almost there when Chloe came into the living room. He held out his arms, and she walked right into them. Her arms circled his waist, and he felt her shudder.

"I'm sorry," he murmured, his face in her hair.

She held on tighter. So did he.

Zack felt his mother and Carmen brush past, but his mind was on Chloe and the strawberry scent of her hair.

"Chloe, darling," his mother said in a whisper, as

if she didn't want to disturb. "You were magnificent tonight."

"You were, you know," he said, tipping Chloe's head so he could see her eyes.

"Thank you, Zack." Chloe loved having him hold her like this. The poison of her father's words seemed to fade as she stayed in Zack's arms.

"Okay, you two," Cate called out way too soon. "It's too quiet out here."

"Come talk to us," Carmen added. "We're all traumatized."

They'd left the love seat for Zack and herself, which was thoughtful. If Chloe couldn't have his arms around her, at least she could feel him near, and she still held his hand.

"Could I begin by saying how grateful I am for all of you?" Chloe said. "I heard what you said to Dad as I was leaving, and you were great!"

"It was long overdue," Carmen said curtly.

"You know there will be reprisals," Chloe warned.

"Bring them on," Cate said. "All of our lives we've known that Mom and Dad treated you differently, and I'm sick of it."

"Then I haven't imagined it?" Chloe said without thinking.

"No," her sisters said in unison.

"As the oldest," Carmen said, "I'd like to take a stab at the explanation."

Chloe would love to hear Carmen's take on this, but she glanced at Bonnie and Zack. "Should we be burdening the Hemingways with this?"

"That's up to you, Chloe," Carmen said.

"I'd like to be included if you don't mind," Bonnie said.

Zack just squeezed her hand and said, "I'm already family. Your parents said so." The twinkle in his eye broadened the definition of family. Chloe gave Carmen a nod to go ahead.

Carmen began by turning to Bonnie. "Bonnie, my birth father died in a car accident a month before I was born."

"I'm so sorry!"

"It wasn't a problem for me. My dad—Sterling—supposedly fell in love with baby Carmen before he fell for Mom. He adopted me, and I always felt I had a loving father."

"And Carmen's lived her whole life trying to please him," Cate said dryly. "Mom and I talk about it all the time."

"Cate and her mother are as close as Carmen and her father are," Zack said as an aside to his mother.

"Who was close with Chloe?" Bonnie asked, an eyebrow raised.

Chloe had to smile. She knew that eyebrow, and it felt good, knowing she had someone on her side.

Carmen sighed. "You would have thought our parents would have been gaga over Chloe, their first daughter together, and they probably were, but Dad wasn't home much, and Mom was immediately pregnant again."

"I'm not sure when they realized Chloe was extra smart," Cate said. "My early memories are of Mom entertaining women friends while Carmen and I played together and watched *Mr. Rogers* on TV."

"What was Chloe doing?" Bonnie asked.

Cate shrugged. "Reading. She liked the big books Mom had on the shelf to impress people. Chloe liked to talk about what she read, but nobody wanted to listen. That's when she was sent to a preschool for the gifted. Right, Chloe?"

She nodded. She'd been a sponge for information. That had been her little life.

"We all knew Spanish from the maid and Mom's family," Carmen added, "but Chloe picked up Japanese from a little girl in the neighborhood, Portuguese from the pool guy and bits of other languages from her school."

Bonnie took a deep breath. "Have you heard this before, Zack?"

Chloe wondered about that, too. In her adult years, she'd made an effort to keep her IQ from making her noticeably different. Would Zack's feelings for her change now that he knew she was—and always had been—different?

"I'd gotten the drift that Chloe wasn't your average middle child," he said, "but the past isn't as important to me as the present. I like the woman sitting beside me just as she is."

That was the perfect thing to say. Chloe squeezed his hand.

"Bonnie, you would not believe what a strange, adorable child Chloe was," Carmen said. "She still had her baby teeth when she knew the purpose of her chewable vitamins, and she could pronounce pharmaceutical terms with ease. Dad would describe his surgeries to her using technical terms, and it was like inputting data to a little computer. To entertain his friends, he'd have her repeat it, word for word. And she could."

"Sterling would have enjoyed that," Bonnie said softly. "Roland, my husband, was so pleased when Zack showed interest in the things he liked."

"Which wasn't very often," Zack said, hating the memories.

"Dad *did* enjoy Chloe's gift," Carmen said, "but one day this little girl had the audacity to say she wasn't going to be a doctor. She wanted to work with children."

"Did our roof fall in that day," Cate asked dryly, "or do I just remember it that way?"

"Nothing could change Chloe's mind," Carmen said. "Dad was furious."

"That never made sense to me," Chloe said, remembering how bewildered she'd been at the time. "I loved working with kids. They don't treat you like a freak if you happen to be smart."

"That's what drew you to children?" Zack asked, looking at her with interest.

"Maybe, I'm not sure. I like to believe it was the Lord's leading."

"And it could have been." Carmen nodded. "But Mom and Dad took it personally when they realized your IQ wasn't going to be an asset to them. If you'd used your genius in the medical world, Dad could have gloated endlessly about where you got your DNA."

Chloe wondered why she'd never thought of that. But if that explained why she wasn't close with her parents, how could she bridge the gap?

* * *

Zack hadn't wanted to leave Chloe, but his mom had the big trip back home tomorrow. Back at his condo, Mom had gone to her room. He'd changed into a pair of shorts and a T-shirt, then stretched out on his leather couch to watch the news and try to settle his mind.

There was a drive-by shooting somewhere and some senator was in trouble for something. Zack heard the words, but they didn't get through to him. He couldn't stop thinking about Chloe, and he couldn't wait to see her again.

She had to work in the morning, and he had to take Mom to the airport. But later, he wanted to take Chloe to a place where they could talk and be totally alone. The ocean would be good. There were miles of beaches and little coves.

He turned the TV off. Too much had happened tonight for him to care about the weather forecast or sports. One thing for sure, he would never feel the same about Sterling and Ava, and that was too bad. They'd been good to him, but if they weren't *very* good to Chloe, he wouldn't be getting together with them.

He knew what he felt for Chloe now. He loved her. He waited to feel like a fool, but he didn't. He just wanted to say it out loud, again and again, and he would…when Mom wasn't in the next room.

It wasn't rational, this feeling he had for Chloe. His approach to life was thoughtful and scientific. He'd never trusted an instinct this strong with so little to back it up. Decisions about personal matters weren't made in a hurry. People didn't fall in love so quickly.

Yet here he was, wishing Chloe were beside him.

Mom came out of the spare bedroom. She'd changed into her pajamas and taken off her makeup. She did look older without it, but she was still the prettiest mom a guy ever had.

"Zack, I have something I need to talk to you about. I'd planned to tell you earlier this week, but I couldn't, and now, here it is, my last night here…." Her voice trailed off.

"It's okay, Mom," he said automatically, but this couldn't be good.

"I hate to give you more to think about." She sank down on the couch beside him and reached for his hand.

He could do better than that. He put his arm around her and tucked her close. Her body seemed to shake. Was she about to tell him that she was ill, despite her denials? "What's going on, Mom?"

"I've been dreading this moment from the day you were born. No, even before you were born."

"It's okay, Mom," he said again, wanting to ease her distress.

"Oh, Zack, it's really not okay. I'm afraid you'll hate me."

"I could never hate you!" How could she think that?

"I pray that you don't. Darling, I've loved you since the day I knew you were going to be mine. You needed me to make good decisions, but I was going through the most confusing, deeply unhappy time of my life. I'd loved your father with all of my heart, and I'd believed him when he said we would be married. When I told him we were going to have you, he said you couldn't be his! I'd never been with another man! He said we were through, and he meant it. From that day on he wouldn't see me or take my calls. It was just you and me."

Emotions welled up inside Zack, one tumbling over another—rage that Mom had experienced such betrayal…contempt for the man who had done that to her…and a horrible sense of relief. Roland Hemingway couldn't have been his father.

"Your birth father came from a wealthy, influential family, but I couldn't risk losing you by turning to them. So I prayed and went home to my parents. My mother cried with me when I told her about you. We went to a very strict church. We both knew that my father would say I couldn't stay. I would be a bad example for our young people."

"And putting you out on the street came from what part of the Bible?" Zack couldn't help the anger in his voice.

"Roland's parents were members of the same church. When he heard I was pregnant, he said he'd always loved me, and he would marry me. It didn't matter that I wasn't in love with him or that his parents turned their back on him, too. We moved to the Midwest and never saw them again."

He nodded as if he understood, but he didn't. Was there anything or anyone a person could completely count on?

"The only thing Roland asked of me was that my baby would be raised as his. That was little enough to give him when he was giving me so much."

So, that was why Mom had been so tolerant of Dad's moods. It had been his hold over her.

"When you were little, Roland loved you as if you were his."

And that was Zack's memory.

"But when you became older and wanted no part of his world, he took it hard. Do you remember how much he loved fixing cars? Every time he went to the store, he would bring you back a little car. He would have played with you, but you would set the new car on your windowsill with the others and go back to taking care of some bird or squirrel in your hospital. Roland would look at you and say, 'He's not mine, Bonnie. He'll never be mine.'"

Zack could see how that would hurt, but did it justify the man's anger? Zack had never known when his dad's temper would explode and he would smash the little cars with his foot.

"When you showed such passion to become a doctor, Roland became more and more angry. You not only looked like your birth father, you had his interests." She took a worn picture from her purse. "Zack, this is your birth father. You know him well."

Without looking at the picture, he would guess it was Albert Brennan. The man had been like a father to him, but it was impossible to imagine Albert getting a young woman pregnant and abandoning her.

"Recognize him, Zack?"

It looked like Collin. It looked like himself.

Zack wanted to throw up.

Chapter Fourteen

His birth father was Charlie Brennan?

The man was a good urologist, but Zack hadn't liked him before, and he sure didn't now. How many other half brothers and sisters did he have out there? Hot anger had him off the sofa and pacing the floor. He clenched and unclenched his hands, wanting to settle the score for what Charlie had done to Mom.

"I'm sorry, Zack," his mom said tearfully.

For once in his life, he didn't automatically reassure her. It wasn't her fault, but he hated this!

"I'm sorry I was naive about Charlie," she said. "I'm sorry I couldn't find a way to stop Roland's meanness, and, most of all, I'm sorry for not telling you before now. I wanted to, and I asked Roland to release me from my promise many times, but he would always say no. I think keeping the truth from you was his revenge for a life that didn't turn out as he'd hoped."

Would it have mattered if Zack had known who his

birth father was? It might have. For sure, he would have steered clear of the Brennans, and he might have felt less like a loser if he'd known where his dad's hatred came from.

His dad. How sad that Roland had wanted to be a good dad, but he'd been beaten by Charlie's undeniable DNA. Zack really did feel like throwing up. He didn't want to be either man's son.

"Zack, do you hate me?" Tears flowed down her cheeks.

He'd been so caught up in his reaction that he wasn't thinking how awful this must be for her. "No, Mom, I could never hate you. Don't even think such a thing." He pulled her from the sofa to hold her.

She clutched his shoulders as if she feared losing him.

It would never happen. "Mom, I'm just processing what you had to go through to give me a home. You're my mom, and I love you."

She cried, and he had to blink back tears. Both of them had carried a lot of pain for a long time.

When the first wave of emotion ebbed and Mom had pulled it together, Zack asked, "Mom, who else knows this?"

"I'm not sure. Remember what Albert said at the hospital? That when he met you, he thought you were the spitting image of a relative of his? I knew he was talking about Charlie."

"He must have been," Zack said, wiped out that he hadn't caught the hint from Albert. If Albert knew, who else did?

Fresh tears welled in Mom's eyes. "When you were

invited to join Brennan Medical Clinic at such a young age, I knew this had to be Charlie's family, but I didn't know if they'd told you the truth, or if you'd put it together."

"Obviously I hadn't. I thought I was so good at my work that they invited me there. I'll be rethinking all that. Mom, was my connection with the Brennans why you and Dad never visited me?"

"Yes." Her sigh was huge. "I'd made that promise to your dad. To keep it, I had to bury my head in the sand and deny what was right so many times."

"This week must have been so hard on you." He thought of the times her face had gone ashen and how she'd tried to avoid the Brennans.

Anger flared in her eyes. "The worst moment was seeing Charlie's picture on the Brennan Medical Clinic wall and thinking how he'd denied you. You're *his* son, Zack, not an honorary Brennan through the kindness of Albert and his wife."

"Albert…he's my uncle," Zack said as if he'd just wakened from a dream. He'd been so caught up in the unfairness of events and all his mother had suffered that he hadn't thought of the big picture. "And Collin's my brother!" Beth, Ry and Trey Brennan were his cousins; their dad was his uncle and he had two aunts. He had a huge family.

Or not.

He could walk away from his Brennan connection. Did he really want to be part of a family that included Charlie Brennan? "Do all of the Brennans know that Charlie is my father?"

"Not from what your grandfather told me yesterday afternoon."

His *grandfather!* The chief, the founder of Brennan Medical Clinic, was his grandfather! "Is that what he wanted to talk to you about?"

She nodded, her eyes brightening. "He's eager to talk to you and acknowledge your true relationship. He's kept it a secret out of respect for me and Roland, but it's time for that secret to come out. It's time you took your rightful place as a Brennan. Nothing should hold you back."

Zack collapsed in a chair. So many things made sense now. There was that wild rumor that he was slated to become head of the clinic someday. It had seemed completely implausible to him. The Brennan grandchildren were the logical candidates for that responsibility, not him. But the chief had known he had another grandchild. Actually, now that Zack thought about it, he was the oldest of the bunch.

"Zack, you have a lot to think about," his mom said.

Talk about an understatement!

She kissed his forehead. "In the worst of times I've claimed the words of Ephesians 3:20. The Lord is able to do far more than we can imagine. Consider His purpose in your life, Zack, and let the Lord bless you."

With a gentle good-night kiss, she left the room.

He was a mess. Could he settle down and focus on God's Word? Right now, it didn't seem like it. His life had been turned upside down, and the only thing he could think of was how much he wished Chloe were here to help him figure this out.

* * *

Zack lay on the sofa and glanced at his watch again. He hadn't gone to bed last night. Since dawn, he'd been waiting to call Chloe. He felt so angry, but he hoped she could find the positive side of this mess. If anyone could, it would be her.

He hoped it was late enough to call. He dialed her phone.

"Well, good morning," she said in a sleepy voice.

"Did I wake you?"

"I should be up and getting ready for work." He heard a soft yawn. "Excuse me, but I didn't sleep well last night. I sort of prayed and dozed on and off all night."

His night had been like that, too, except his sequence had three parts—praying, dozing and thinking about being a Brennan.

"What time does Bonnie's flight leave?" Chloe asked.

"A little before eleven. We'll head to LAX and have breakfast before she boards."

"What are you going to do on the last day of your vacation?"

Think about you. Think about me being a Brennan. Think about the two of us moving to the Midwest to get away from your parents and my new family. "We have a date when you get off work, right?

"We do! A real unchaperoned date!"

He could hear the joy in her voice, and it did make him feel better. "Are you one of those women who feels disrespected if the guy doesn't have everything planned for the date, or are you okay with spontaneous decisions about what we do?"

"You have to ask? My whole life is spontaneous. Cate would expect the guy to have everything planned. Carmen would probably prefer to plan the date herself."

She knew her sisters well.

"But I go with the flow and live in the moment. I might be self-conscious if I were in jeans and you showed up in a suit, but give me five minutes to change, and I'm good to go. Whatever we do tonight, we're going to have a good time."

That eliminated his plan to tell her about the Brennans. "Do you want to set the dress code for tonight?" he asked, almost sure of what she would say.

"Casual is good. I'll bring a sweater just in case we want to watch the sun set and the moon come up at the beach. I loved that night with your mom."

It was the night he'd known he'd have trouble holding on to his single life.

They talked a little more, but she didn't mention the trauma at her parents' house and he didn't mention Mom's big news. She ended the call, saying how much she looked forward to their date. He said something equally generic, but he wished he'd had the guts to say what he really felt—that he didn't know how he could wait until late afternoon to see her.

How long would it be? He did the simple math. Nine hours. Some of his surgeries ran that long and the time flew.

Mom was moving about in her room, and he should get ready. It would make her nervous if they didn't get to the airport early. She would rather sit in the boarding area by herself than risk being late.

He'd showered and was shaving, comparing his features to Charlie's and Collin's, when his cell phone rang. Out of habit he checked the caller ID before he answered. What he saw was better than sunshine. He could hardly flip the phone open fast enough.

"Chloe!" It didn't matter that he smeared shaving cream on the phone.

"Zack, I feel pretty foolish calling you back—"

Oh, no! Was she going to cancel?

"It isn't like me to do this, but I was just wondering—"

He held his breath, waiting for the other shoe to fall.

"Would you like to get together for lunch?"

His emotions were so raw he felt the sting of tears behind his eyes.

"Don't feel like you have to," she said. "I mean, we're getting together tonight, but—"

"Yes," he said firmly, cutting her off. "I was wondering how I could wait until this evening to see you again." There, he'd said it.

He heard her take a quick breath. "I felt that way, too."

Chloe spent the morning reading and answering mail, but her mind was on the beautiful red roses on her desk—and the man who'd sent them. The card read, "Love, Zack." That made her heart sing.

Her life had become very complicated since she'd been home. On the plus side were her sisters and Zack. On the minus side were…her sisters and Zack.

They'd supported her unconditionally and she appreciated them more than words could say, but it bothered her terribly that they'd placed themselves in Dad's line of fire. Carmen had a valued relationship with Dad, and as chief of surgery, Dad could help or hinder Zack's career. Was there a way she could make up for that or somehow distance herself from them so Dad's wrath would be on her and not them?

Distance could be good, especially from Zack. By nature she was impulsive and a risk taker, but she didn't want to lose her heart to him without knowing for sure that he was the one God meant for her.

Intuition said he might let her into his life, but she couldn't see Zack parenting a brood of adopted children, nor could she see him sitting back and letting her do that alone.

Maybe she wasn't meant to have children at all. Maybe the Lord's purpose for her life was to encourage thousands of others to step up and pay more attention to kids. Maybe she was to be the voice of all children instead of listening to little voices that she adored in her own home.

Could Zack be The One? The question came back again and again. She cared about him so much.

Lord, one more time I surrender my life. One more time I bring Zack to You, and I ask that You remove him from my life if he's not The One. Take him from my life quickly, like tape ripped from skin, so the hurt will be less, and I'll forget about the loss. Or…convince me that he's mine to love…whatever happens.

Zack played with her fingers as they waited for their lunch to be prepared. "I'm going to miss you."

"Are you going somewhere?" she asked, hoping her dismay didn't show.

He smiled briefly to acknowledge her comment, but his eyes didn't make the effort. "I'm not going anywhere, but my vacation ends tonight. My routine begins with an early morning surgery and, if all goes well, I'll make it home in time to go to bed and start it all over again the next day. I won't have time for lunches like this."

He had no idea how resourceful she could be. If she was sure he wanted to be with her, they would find little moments to be together…or this might be God's way of slowing things down between them. She thought she knew Zack pretty well, but she'd only known him while he was on vacation. It would be different when he was back in his regular routine.

"How did you discover this place?" she asked, looking about the dimly lit restaurant. It was a perfect refuge from the bright early May sun. Soft music provided a relaxing background. High-backed booths offered privacy. When she'd slid into one side of the booth, Zack had followed her instead of sitting across from her. It made her feel as though they were a couple.

"Albert took me here one day," Zack said.

"I've always liked Albert Brennan. He and Amy were so sweet last night. Albert's been a wonderful friend to you, hasn't he, Zack?"

Zack let go of her hand and took a sip of his iced tea. She thought he wasn't going to answer, but then he said, "He's been a wonderful uncle."

Uncle? Had she heard him right? Their food arrived;

the waiter topped up their drinks; Zack broke open his dinner roll and buttered it lightly. He forked a bite of salmon and seemed to take forever to eat it.

Moments passed. She couldn't wait any longer. "Albert's been a wonderful *uncle?*"

Zack shoved his plate aside. "Last night Mom broke the news to me that Charlie Brennan is my birth father."

Chloe's heart seemed to stop.

"Mom and Charlie were college students at Stanford. Mom had won a scholarship there. She was so pretty that Charlie singled her out of the pack right away. He was her first love."

"When we were in her hotel suite, she said she'd been so in love with your father. I thought she meant Roland, but—"

"She meant Charlie. Mom came from a strict, religious home. She wouldn't have broken her moral code if she'd realized the kind of man he was...and is."

"The day we had the clown lesson, she mentioned a bad choice she'd made as a young woman...a choice she'd paid for dearly."

"She really did pay," he said, rubbing his hand across his eyes wearily. "When she told Charlie she was pregnant with me, he said it couldn't be his."

Revulsion rose from Chloe's pores. "What a creep!"

How could Bonnie have loved a man who ended up treating her so horribly? How could she speak of loving him as a good experience? People said that love was blind, but could the memory of first love be that distorted?

"She paid again when she went back home. Her parents were good church people, yet they disowned her."

"They didn't," Chloe said in disbelief. Thirty years ago there might have been a bigger taboo for unwed mothers than there was now, but parents didn't disown their children in their greatest time of need.

"Roland Hemingway was a friend from Mom's church. When he said he would marry Mom and raise her baby, his parents dumped him, too. His only condition was that no one should know he was my adopted father."

When Bonnie said she'd paid dearly, she'd understated the price. "Does it help to know that your mom didn't waste much time setting the record straight after Roland died? What a burden she carried all those years."

He nodded, his face grim. "Remember when I said I used to wonder if Madison Haines and I hadn't been switched at birth? The joke was on me. It was the dads who were switched, not the babies. But I've got to feel for Roland. He didn't get the son he expected to raise. Isn't it amazing, Chloe? I knew nothing about Charlie or any of the Brennans, but I've wanted to be a doctor as long as I can remember."

"It makes a strong case for genetics over environment."

"But environment played its part. It was Albert who influenced me to follow him into his specialty. I keep wondering what I would have done if my path hadn't crossed his. He didn't know about me. He only recognized a familiar face. Charlie didn't tell any of his family. For all I know, Collin and I might have other siblings that Charlie denied."

"You might," she agreed. "And it might not have

been a coincidence that your paths crossed. Your mom and I believe in God's direction, not chance."

"Chloe, do you really think it was God's plan that Roland would end up hating my guts? Was it God's plan that I would end up with a family who's known about me for a decade and said nothing about it?"

The pain in those questions made her feel ill. It would have to be addressed, but not now.

He glanced at his watch. "Forget I said that. I'm just blowing off steam. Please, go ahead, eat your lunch."

She took up her fork. "Okay, but I'm not eating alone." She pushed his plate back in front of him.

There was a glimmer of a smile on his face when he took another bite of his salmon and followed that with a gulp of iced tea. His eyes were on her, and she could tell he was trying harder to smile. In the midst of this horrible time, his effort was no little thing. If she hadn't been in love with him before, she was now.

It was no time to tell him, though. If he didn't feel the same way, that would be just one more problem for him. She was here as his friend—someone he could count on. That's all.

Chapter Fifteen

He dropped her off at work and Chloe went straight to the restroom where she could be alone. "I love him," she said out loud, trying out the words in front of the mirror. "I love Zack Hemingway. What do you think about that?"

The woman in the mirror glowed with happiness for her.

"Should I tell him?" Chloe asked.

The woman in the mirror frowned and cocked her head as if she were thinking about it.

"If he's not ready to hear it, he might back away just when he needs a friend. Right?"

The mirrored reflection didn't argue.

In Chloe's book, that was a confirmation. She would just brush her teeth, floss, and wait for the Lord to give her the right words at the right time. Zack had so much new information in his life, he didn't need more.

After work, she rushed home, showered and changed into jeans and her prettiest top. A glance at the mirror said she could do better. She switched the jeans for a jeans skirt and brought out the eyelash curler and mascara.

She was pacing Carmen's driveway and praying for Zack when he showed up. At first glance, she was alarmed. He looked so much worse than he had at lunch. Defeat was stamped on his face and his eyes looked so tired. Impulsively, she hurried to his side of the car and motioned for him to get out.

Zack picked up on Chloe's urgency and was out of the car almost before the motor shut down. Her arms were around him in a fierce hug before his feet hit the pavement. The hug couldn't have come at a better time. He'd spent the entire afternoon doubting all of his relationships and wondering what people would think if they learned he was a Brennan. Chloe left no question about how she felt, and that was healing medicine to his troubled mind.

She stroked his neck as if to say everything was going to be all right. If she cared this much, everything *would* be okay. When she kissed him, he closed his eyes and forgot about everything except how much he loved Chloe.

A car horn tooted and Carmen called out, "Sorry to interrupt, but I've driven around the block twice. I'd like to park my car."

"Ignore her," Chloe murmured against his cheek.

He smiled inside and sort of danced Chloe and himself out of Carmen's path.

"Is there anything I can get you two?" Carmen asked on her way to the house. "Soda? Sandwich? Lip balm?"

"Nothing for me," Chloe murmured.

"I'm good," he added.

"Let me guess," Carmen said dryly. "You're going for some kind of record—like 'couple with the highest combined IQ doing the dumbest thing possible'? You do realize that my neighbor is the wife of BMC's operating manager, and this public display of affection will be all over the clinic grapevine by noon tomorrow and the hospital rumor mill will have it not long after?"

He didn't care about that, but he broke their kiss. "Have you got a minute, Carmen? There's something I'd like to ask you."

The woman in his arms looked at him with curious eyes, but she didn't move an inch from his side.

"Do you want to come inside?" Carmen asked.

He shook his head. "It's just a yes-or-no kind of question."

"Fire away," Carmen said, walking toward them.

"Okay. Do you know I'm Charlie Brennan's son?"

She registered no surprise, and her eyes went to Chloe.

"She knows!" Chloe exclaimed, just as shocked as he was.

"And now you both know," Carmen said with a relieved sigh. "Make a note. Never promise you'll keep a secret until you know what it is. Zack, I have felt terrible, but I couldn't tell you. I can't apologize enough. I haven't told a soul. Cate doesn't know. Neither do Mom or Dad."

"You're kidding!" Zack was really surprised by that. "Albert and your dad are such good friends. I figured Albert told him when it looked like I might make a play for Beth."

"You almost had it right. Albert bypassed Dad and took me into his confidence so I'd try to get your attention. Albert thought you might be getting too interested in your cousin. I was supposed to distract you, but I soon learned that you weren't that interested in Beth *or* me. Chloe, this guy does not fall for just any girl, and it isn't every day he kisses a woman he barely knows on my front lawn."

Zack cleared his throat and smiled sheepishly. "All evidence to the contrary."

"Exactly! So is it the real thing between you two?"

Chloe looked at Zack, wondering what he would say. He seemed to be waiting for her to answer. She might as well tell the truth and see what happened.

"Zack's my boyfriend," she said. If he wanted to correct that, she could claim she was teasing, but his quick grin said he remembered the boyfriend-girlfriend status they'd agreed on in Solvang.

"You don't think you're moving a little fast?" Carmen teased, or maybe that was her way of posing a serious question without sounding parental.

"It's not fast compared to the overnight discovery that I'm a Brennan," Zack said dryly.

"And it's not fast considering everyone in my family has known you for two years," Chloe said. "They can vouch for you."

"They may not want to if they find out I'm Charlie's son." Zack's lip curled in disgust.

"If?" Carmen repeated. "Are you considering keeping it a secret? You don't want to be recognized as a Brennan?"

"I don't know. I haven't had as long to think about it as you have." He smiled to take the sting out of the comment, but Chloe saw Carmen flinch. Poor Carmen. The secret had put her in a terrible position.

Zack grabbed Chloe's hand and led her toward his car. "Right now, my girlfriend and I are going to hang out at the beach and get some perspective about what's important in this crazy world."

Chloe said over her shoulder, "Carmen, you can tell Cate that I'm Zack's girlfriend. That's not a secret, and you know how she'll love it."

Zack drove to the freeway and said, "I thought we might eat near the beach."

"And watch the sun set?" She could imagine his arms around her as the moon came up. "We could call your mom and give her a play-by-play of the sun-and-moon action," she said to make him smile. "Did Bonnie get home okay?"

"She did, but I could tell she's very worried about the Brennan thing. She and J. T. Brennan had a long talk the day I was talking to you in Denver."

"And…?"

"The chief told her he wants to go public and claim me as a Brennan."

"How do you feel about that?"

"I'm considering a move back to the Midwest. Do you like the Midwest?" he asked with a grin.

He wasn't serious. This was just his way of coping with too much information in too short a time, but she played along. "Sure. I love the seasonal changes… summer, fall, winter, spring…that kind of thing."

"Yeah, me, too. Why put up with year-round sunshine when you can have all that?"

She could talk nonsense all evening if that would help, but if he needed to talk about the serious repercussions of being a Brennan, she could do that, too.

"So, who actually knows about your connection to the Brennans?" she asked.

"As I understand it, it's just the chief, Albert and Amy."

"And Carmen."

"I'm not sure he knows Albert confided in her. When Albert discovered me at Stanford and hired an investigator who proved my relationship, he took that information to the chief."

"Not Charlie?"

Zack made a sound of disgust. "The Brennans have no illusions about Charlie. His indiscretions are legendary. The chief told Mom that he was deeply humiliated when he discovered he had an unclaimed twenty-year-old grandson."

"That rings true," Chloe said. "J. T. Brennan is an honorable man. I can imagine how angry he must have been at Charlie even though it must have been a thrill for him to realize he would have another doctor in the Brennan family."

"At the time, that was no sure thing. I had the grades, but I was a scholarship student with no money for med school. You'll think I'm a little slow, but it was only this afternoon that I realized how much easier my life got after I met Albert. I started getting all this anonymous financial aid. Of course I wondered about it, but the dean said a generous alum wanted to 'pay it forward'—you know, give to a worthy student who would provide for another worthy student down the line. I didn't question it."

"Who would have? It was logical, and you were deserving."

"I didn't suspect Albert Brennan was my benefactor. He was just a man I'd met in a lecture hall. If the chief hadn't told Mom that he began providing for me as the other Brennan grandchildren were provided for, I might never have known. How's that for being dense?"

"I know the feeling. I didn't suspect my parents were providing for me with a payback in mind. Now that I know Dad wants my Ph.D., I feel obligated to get it for him. Do you feel indebted to the Brennans?"

"Well, yeah!" His mouth disappeared into a grim line. "And I'm trying to sort out what I earned on my own and what I got because they made it happen. I graduated first in my class. I don't think they could buy that for me, but I'll never know."

"Could you consider that everything came as God's blessing?"

"Could you accept your parents' support and *not* finish your Ph.D.?"

Ouch. That hit home. "Pride has its price, doesn't it?"

"Not for everyone," he said knowingly. "If Charlie discovers he has another son, he won't even flinch."

"When is Collin going to be told that he has a brother?" she asked tentatively. It was a loaded question.

"I don't know," Zack said, rubbing the back of his

neck. "But I can't be the one to do it. I would have loved to have grown up with Collin."

From the way Zack was rubbing his neck, he must be in pain. She reached over, felt the taut cords and began a gentle massage.

He took a deep breath. "That feels great." He continued taking long, deep breaths to let his tension go. After a few minutes, she thought she should take her hand away, but he murmured, "Don't stop."

And she didn't until he said, "That's enough. I know you're tired."

The ocean came into view, and the vastness of it impressed her all over again. When she saw the might of God's creation, it was impossible to think there was a problem He couldn't solve.

Zack parked at a seafood restaurant and turned in his seat to face her. He swept a few strands of hair from her face with a touch so gentle, she drew in a quick breath. Gone from his eyes was that sad, intense look, and in its place was an expression so loving she struggled to breathe.

"Chloe, about what Carmen said…do you think we're moving too fast?"

She swallowed hard. "If it were someone other than me, I might think so, but I've never…moved too fast."

"Neither have I."

His big, wide smile was the one she liked best.

"My mother loves you, and I'm practically family according to your father. I'm thirty-one, and you're twenty-eight. We're better educated than most. We know what we want in life—"

"And we both know how to pray. That's big, Zack."

"It is, isn't it? Would you believe I pray for you all the time? I wasn't a guy who prayed a lot before I heard you speak at the conference. What you do is so important, Chloe."

Happiness was such a fluttery, beautiful feeling. "That's a nice thing to say."

"Get used to hearing nice things. You deserve them."

The man definitely knew how to make a woman's heart race. If she didn't get out of the car now, she would have to kiss him again.

In the restaurant, he sat beside her in a booth, just as he had at lunch. It was extra effort to concentrate on reading the menu instead of looking at Zack. "What are you having?" she asked.

"I'm not sure yet," he said, claiming her hand.

She loved the way he did that, and she loved the feel of his thumb stroking hers. Maybe she should order fish and chips. That only required one hand. She could nibble while she concentrated on the man.

But she ordered grilled tuna and an interesting salad. Zack said he'd have the same. He hadn't even checked the menu. "Do you like Gorgonzola cheese and Granny Smith apples? They're in the salad."

"Is that what we're having? Cool. I can eat anything."

"Why did you order what I did?"

"I can't tell you. You'd laugh."

"I hope so. Tell me."

"Not tonight."

"When then?"

"Someday."

"So it's a secret?"

"No!" he said sharply. "I don't have secrets. I'll tell you, but please don't freak out."

"Have you ever seen me 'freak out'?" she asked dryly.

He studied her face, and his eyes softened. "No, I haven't. You know, one of the things I like best about you is how you can find the positive side of the worst situation, and you have a great sense of humor."

"That's two things." Compliments always threw her. "But who's counting?"

His smile was so approving, she might melt to the floor. She'd waited all of her life for this feeling.

"I ordered the same thing you did because it makes me feel like we're a couple—a couple who've sat at the same table year after year, eating meals that one of us cooked."

Tears stung at the back of her eyes. He saw them together forever? A man who professed to love his life just as it was?

But today Zack wasn't himself. She would love to sit at that table with him, but she should keep this light. "Do you cook, Zack, or should one of us learn?"

"Maybe," he said, smiling as she hoped, "though I doubt that we have the time right now. My vacation ends tonight, and you'll be working on your dissertation soon."

"Tomorrow I have an appointment with my research adviser. I did the course work for my Ph.D. before I was twenty. I've gone beyond the time limit to complete it, but I applied for extensions along the way. I dread doing the work, but I can't wait to put the finished product in Dad's hands."

He nodded and there was a glint in his eyes. "I'd like to be there for that."

"You will be," she promised.

Their food came. They agreed that the salads were awesome and Chloe could order for them both from now on.

The sun was setting when they strolled along the beach looking for a spot where the sounds of others wouldn't reach them. A storm might be approaching because the wind was up and the waves crashed ashore.

They spread their blanket and sat arm in arm, their heads together, watching the orange-gold sky fade to the pastels of dusk. Sometimes they talked. Sometimes long minutes passed before they spoke again.

She let Zack take the lead in what they discussed. Occasionally he talked about the same thing, retracing what had already been said. That was how unsettled he was.

The situation bothered him in so many ways, but the thing that seemed to bother him most was the length of time Albert and J. T. Brennan had known about him. "Chloe, how could they hold a secret that big and for so long? Mom says my grandfather—it doesn't feel right to call the chief that—is eager to establish a family relationship with me. She reminds me that he's elderly and hints of his limited time on this earth, but he's known he was my grandfather eleven years! We've worked under the same roof the last two! What's the hurry now?"

"He *is* getting older."

"I know, but then what's Albert's excuse? He let me think he was my friend and mentor. Now he wants to be my uncle? I don't shift gears this fast."

She was holding a big secret herself. That she couldn't have biological children might not be as big to him as it was to her, but she'd have to tell him if they were going to be a couple. Tonight he had enough to think about. "Zack, don't you think their delay in telling you had more to do with your mother's feelings than anything else? She'd made a life for herself. They wouldn't have wanted to make her life harder than Charlie had done."

He released a deep, pent-up sigh. "I know."

"They could have sealed that can of worms and tried to forget about you. Who would have known the difference? But what did they do? Albert and his wife took it upon themselves to watch over you and treat you like their own."

"I know." He nodded. "It's irrational, but I feel trapped. I owe them so much, I couldn't walk away if I wanted to."

"Think about Collin. He's just as trapped, only he's had to deal with Charlie all these years."

The corner of his mouth lifted in a small smile, but almost immediately shut down. "Chloe, I don't want anyone to know I'm Charlie Brennan's son."

"Of course you don't, but it won't be as bad as you may think. Collin's survived it. You will, too."

He kissed her forehead. "That's what I love about you. You see the good when I can't see anything but bad."

There was still an edge of bitterness in his voice, but he'd had enough Brennan-talk for one day. It was enough to sit beside him and let him feel she was there for him. The awesome power of the ocean was a reminder that no matter what happened, they were not alone. The great Creator still had them in mind.

Chapter Sixteen

Zack changed into his scrubs and got ready for his first surgery since his vacation. Usually he felt a thrill of anticipation, knowing he was about to change someone's life for the better, but not today. It was inevitable that he would see some of the Brennans. He wasn't ready to be outed as one of them, but how much of a strain would it be to continue the lie?

And then there was Chloe. She was on his mind all the time. He could almost smell the strawberry scent of her long dark hair and see her expressive dark eyes.

Collin strolled into the lounge and took a step back. "Whoa! I thought you'd look rested, but when have you slept, man?"

In the last forty-eight hours, not much. "You know how it is with vacations," he said, making up a plausible explanation. "You get used to staying up at night. Your sleep cycle is off."

It was the first time Zack had seen Collin since he'd

found out they were brothers. How could he keep it from Collin? The guy was his best friend.

Collin leaned against a locker with his arms folded. "I hear you have quite a dilemma."

Zack sucked in his breath. Who'd told Collin?

"Don't look as if you don't know what I'm talking about," Collin teased.

How could Collin joke about discovering they were brothers?

"It's all over the hospital how you stood up for Chloe at her parents' house. You may have had Sterling's favor before, but not now!"

On an ordinary weekend, the blowup at the Kilgannons *would* have been on Zack's mind, but the discovery that he was Charlie Brennan's son was so much bigger that Zack had almost forgotten he'd had a problem with Sterling.

He thought they were alone in the lounge, but Zack lowered his voice anyway. "Have you seen how Sterling treats Chloe? It's awful."

Collin looked around for extra listeners before he spoke as Zack had. "You know how Sterling likes things his way. He had expectations for his genius daughter, but she had goals of her own. He's tried to bully her in the past, and when she stood up for herself, he called her selfish and stubborn. I'm surprised he hasn't realized he won't win. Chloe's got a soft heart, but when she digs in her heels, she won't let anyone push her around."

"I haven't seen that." He liked the idea of her being strong. If they were going to have a life together—and he thought they were heading that way—she'd be on her own a lot.

"Chloe's a loner—not your typical loner since she gravitates toward kids, but she has this way of keeping to herself, probably to avoid conflict and keep her cool."

That, he would believe.

"So, what are you going to do with a woman like Chloe?" Collin asked with a grin.

"You mean, other than fall for her?"

Collin's eyes lit up. "So the rumor's true. If you were willing to go up against Sterling, I thought Chloe must have gotten to you."

Zack grinned. "She did."

"Seriously, that's great!"

They walked to the OR with Collin giving him advice on how to handle women. Zack pretended to listen, but he couldn't stop thinking that Collin was his brother, and somebody had to tell him soon.

Hours later, Zack backed away from the surgery table and smiled behind his mask. Already the elation that followed every successful surgery was working through his mind. So keen a feeling, as addictive as any drug, it swept over him, a rejuvenating force. Was it any wonder that surgery was his life?

"Nice work, Zack," Collin said from his position as anesthesiologist.

"Good job, everyone," Zack fired back.

They headed for the cafeteria to grab a bite before the next surgery. They'd just found their table when Collin said, "Don't look now, but here comes Sterling."

Sterling wore a gray shirt and pants under his white lab coat. He carried a specialty-label coffee container and looked like the important man he was.

"Gentlemen," he said affably, sitting at their table as if there had been no ugly words two days ago. "Did your mother get home all right, Zack?"

Zack took a bite of his sandwich and nodded. Having a mouth full of food would keep him out of the conversation.

"We missed you Sunday night, Collin," Sterling said, laying on guilt.

"Sorry about that. We had a family birthday. I called Ava and told her."

"Then we'll see you next week," Sterling said firmly. "And you, too, Zack."

Zack finished chewing, swallowed and took a sip of water, stalling to give himself time to think. He wouldn't go without Chloe. "Will your daughters be there?"

"Carmen won't disappoint her dad. Cate won't let her mother down. I can't speak for Chloe." Sterling's lip curled while speaking her name.

Zack's contempt for the man had his stomach in knots. "I'm afraid I don't understand your animosity towards Chloe. I would think any man would be proud to claim her as a daughter."

"You don't know her as well as you think you do," Sterling said, rising from the table.

Zack rose, too. "I know her well enough to know she's a terrific woman."

"Of course she's terrific. She *is* my daughter, but

wait until you're counting on her, and she decides to do what she wants, regardless of how it affects you. Come talk to me then." He took a few steps from the table, then retraced his steps. "Zack, I don't believe we'll look for you at the house this Sunday."

Zack nodded. He hadn't planned to attend anyway.

"But you'll be back," Sterling said with a knowing look.

He walked out of earshot, and Collin let out a deep sigh. "Where do you get the guts to talk to Sterling Kilgannon like that?"

Zack sat back down and ate more of his sandwich. "I'll move out of L.A. before I worry about his favor. Nothing's holding me here except Chloe."

Collin cleared his throat extra loud.

"Okay, and you," Zack amended. It was true. He would miss Collin. Even more, he would miss the chance to find out what it was like to have a brother.

Two and a half hours later, Zack parked his Mercedes in the physicians' lot and stared at Brennan Medical Clinic. It felt like home, and he loved everything about it—the tall palms overhead, the Spanish design of the building, the interior layout that made it so convenient to practice good medicine…and the friends. He'd made a lot of good friends here, including most of the Brennans.

Sure, he could leave his problems behind and head out of town, but it would take more than unexpected Brennan DNA and a spat with Sterling Kilgannon to rattle his cage. He wasn't leaving this place.

On the way to his office, he didn't run into any of

the Brennans, though he knew that Albert was working in the suite they shared. Zack had just changed his suit jacket for a lab coat when his nurse, Marsha, peeked her head into his office.

"Doctor, the chief called and asked if he could have an hour of your time. I put him at the end of the day. I hope that's okay. The chief said he would be coming *here* for the appointment."

"That's fine. Thank you, Marsha." Zack could pretend there was no earth-shattering news he and the chief needed to discuss. Marsha had worked at the clinic long before Zack. If the rumor mill had sniffed out his Brennan connection, she would know it. "What's hot on the grapevine today, Marsha?"

There was a twinkle in her blue eyes. "Do you really want to know? I'm afraid it's all about you."

Zack's heart seemed to stop. Everyone knew?

"The word is you've made your choice of the Kilgannon sisters, and your mother put her stamp of approval on Chloe. Good job, Doctor!"

Zack hid his relief with a grin. Marsha would take that as acknowledgment of his feelings for Chloe, but he didn't mind that. Chloe was his girlfriend and he didn't care who knew it.

J. T. Brennan sat alone in Zack's office, praying for words to atone for Charlie's sin. He didn't expect this meeting to be easy, but now that Zack's mother had given him the go-ahead, it was time…so far past time…to acknowledge his grandchild.

At the sound of Zack at the door, J.T. used the chair

arms to push himself to his feet. He should be standing when he came face-to-face with his grandson.

"Chief, it's good to see you," Zack said, extending his hand as if this were just any meeting.

J.T. wanted to go past the handshake and take the boy into his arms, but if his grandchild needed to maintain the pretense of a professional relationship, he understood. Wasn't that what he himself had done these past two years? He took Zack's hand and held on. This was a moment to prolong. He looked into Zack's blue eyes, and it was like looking back in time. "Do people say you have your mother's eyes?"

The comment seemed to surprise Zack, but he nodded.

"That's because they don't know Charlie. You have his eyes, Zack, and his are like mine—or they were when mine weren't watery with age." The strength in his legs was almost gone, and he leaned heavily on his cane.

Zack may have noticed because he took his arm and said, "Why don't we sit down?"

He would, but not before he'd had a chance to embrace this good boy, this exceptional man. "Zack, I hope you'll—"

Tears clogged his throat and all he could do was open his arms to the grandchild who'd been denied his birthright too long. Would Zack forgive the past? He wouldn't blame Zack if he couldn't.

Zack saw the worry in his grandfather's age-worn face. Mom's parents and Roland's had wanted no part of the child she'd carried, but this grandparent did. Why question the timing? Why not accept love when it was offered?

He took his grandfather into his arms. His grandfather. The very word…it was overwhelming to him. He could love this giant of a man, so frail in his arms. He could choose to accept this new family as his own. Love didn't have to be a random act over which he had no control. It would take guts to be a Brennan at this stage of his life, but when it came to love, he would take all he could get.

Seconds later, maybe minutes, his grandfather patted him on the back and broke their embrace to reach for his chair. Zack sat beside him, so moved by this experience he couldn't speak.

"I'm sorry about many things, Zack," his grandfather said in a voice gruff with emotion. "One of the things I regret is that your grandma missed getting to know you. She would have loved you. You may have trouble believing it, but I have loved you since I knew of you, and I've thanked God every day that He allowed me to work with you and get to know you."

Zack didn't know what to say. He nodded, though it wasn't enough.

"You are a good man, Zack, full of integrity and wise beyond your years."

"Thank you."

"I expect you realize my health's not good."

Zack nodded again. His grandfather's poor health was general knowledge.

"It eases the heart of an old man to know he's left something good behind. In my case, it's the clinic and my family. For so long I was concerned about who my successor should be. Then you came into our lives, and

I knew it was you. Zack, one of these days, I want to see you lead the clinic."

So the rumor about that was true. How could he protest that he was a surgeon, not an administrator, without sounding ungrateful? "Chief, I appreciate your faith—"

"Call me Grandpa, Zack. That's what your brother and your cousins do. And I know what you're going to say. You're young, and you love being a surgeon, but I'm not asking you to give up anything but time to serve on the board. You'll continue your practice as I did before I retired."

That didn't sound impossible, but he couldn't believe the man would bypass the family whom he'd known so much longer. "But what about your sons and your other grandchildren?"

"James and Albert don't have the skill set needed nor the interest. Neither do James's children—Trey, Ry and Beth. Charlie's son, Collin, isn't a leader. Charlie's bad judgment and lack of conscience make him unsuitable. No, you're the one, Zack. You will lead by example, and you'll make sure that Brennan Medical Clinic retains its reputation for the highest quality of care and the highest caliber of physicians on the West Coast."

His grandfather had thought this through—probably for years. "Does your family know that you want this, Chief?"

"Grandpa, Zack, not Chief."

Zack had to smile. "It's a new word in my vocabulary."

"Yes, but you're quick. You'll get it in no time."

His grandfather smiled back with such affection that Zack's heart seemed to turn over. He hoped he could live up to the faith of this man.

"The family knows my wishes. I discussed my choice with my boys when Albert and I were the only ones who knew about you."

"Do you know how surreal this all sounds?"

"I expect it does. I don't want the rest of the family to learn about all this through the grapevine, so I've taken a bit of a chance and invited them here. They should be arriving at my office within the hour."

"And you're going to tell them…?"

"That you belong to us, if that's all right with you. We've waited many years for your mother's permission to let you know we're your family. We can wait longer."

"I felt terrible this morning keeping the secret from Collin. I was nervous about everyone knowing, but I'm ready now."

"Albert and Amy are waiting in his office across the hall. Why don't you go over and break their suspense? They hoped you were ready to be a Brennan, but none of us were sure."

The door to Albert's office was open and the couple sat on a love seat, holding hands with their heads bowed, their eyes closed. Zack cleared his throat to get their attention. As one, they looked up with anxious hope in their eyes.

He grinned and said the first thing that came to his mind. "I'm looking for my aunt and uncle."

Amy rushed into his arms. Albert jabbed his fist high and shouted, "Yes!"

They'd given and given with no promise of return. How could Zack ever repay their love?

They all moved to his grandfather's big office downstairs. Catered food was there, and the Brennans began to arrive. His grandfather said he'd told Charlie to arrive later, but there was Albert and Amy, Albert's brother, James—a thoracic surgeon, and his daughter, pretty blond Beth—a pediatrician—with her handsome dark-haired husband, Noah. Beth's brother, Ry—an E.R. doc—came with his wife, Meg, and Collin arrived with his wife, Glenda.

Absent were James's wife and older son, Trey—both were estranged from the family—but Trey's wife, Isabel, was there. Also absent were his little second cousins, although one of them he already knew. Noah and Beth's daughter, nine-year-old Kendra, had been his patient the day he'd met Flower.

His grandfather motioned Zack to come stand beside his chair, and Albert stood with them. J.T. got the family's attention and told the story of their discovery of Zack and why they'd kept their secret for so long.

The group showed varying degrees of surprise. Zack kept his eyes on Collin, who held Glenda's hand and showed no emotion, but Zack knew his friend. He was processing this news and wondering where they went from here. Charlie's past affected Collin as much as it did Zack.

When Grandpa finished with "Help me welcome Zack to the family, everyone!" the group applauded and called out words of welcome, but Collin stepped forward, his face fierce with emotion. Zack held his breath…until Collin threw his arms around Zack and buried his face in Zack's neck.

Zack held him tight, his eyes closed, savoring the moment. He had a brother. That was worth the embarrassment of having people know Charlie Brennan was his father.

"I always wanted a brother," Collin said.

"I couldn't ask for a better one." Zack's voice was husky, but then he'd never hugged his brother before.

Glenda worked her way into the hug, and Zack gave her a brotherly kiss on the forehead.

Zack had never been much of a hugger, but now that he was a bona fide Brennan, it seemed that he might get pretty good at it. He liked his new family so much. They enjoyed the caterer's food and talked about celebrating holidays and birthdays together. He knew his world was changing forever.

The room hushed when the last person to be invited showed up. Charlie entered the room wearing golfing attire and a winning smile. Tall, trim, his blond hair streaked with grey, he seemed oblivious to the tension in the room.

"Sorry I'm late," he said. "No cell phones allowed on the golf course. What's the occasion?"

"We're welcoming Zack into the family," J.T. said. "It's time he knew he was a Brennan. He's Bonnie Jorgensen's son, Charlie, and yours."

From the blank look on Charlie's face, he didn't remember Bonnie. Zack could have killed him for that. He waited for embarrassment, shame, remorse—something—to show on Charlie's face, but he just grinned and said, "Well, what do you know!"

Unbelievable! Zack glanced at Collin, and his brother shrugged. The rest of the family were more upset about Charlie's sin than Charlie would ever be.

Collin pulled Zack aside. "Does Chloe know you're my brother?"

Zack nodded, but his heart seemed to drop to his knees. He'd forgotten to call her. He'd promised he would. She should have been here for this once-in-a-lifetime experience. How was he going to explain that he hadn't thought of her until now?

Actually it could have been later if Collin hadn't mentioned her name.

Chapter Seventeen

By nature, Chloe was a patient person, but she wasn't tonight. Not only was it her first day of not seeing or hearing from Zack, she'd been sorting through eight years of research notes. At first, her notes had brought back wonderful memories, but now, hours later, her neck, shoulders and head ached, and she was asking herself how she'd gotten herself into this mess.

It *was* a mess—in every way. Her bedroom looked like a hurricane had gone through it, and she might be doing the work for nothing.

This afternoon her new research adviser had dropped the bomb that so much time had lapsed since Chloe had done her original course work, she might be required to repeat all of it! A waiver *might* be granted because she'd been an exceptional student who'd done exceptional research, but the decision was up to a committee.

Since she wasn't the kind of person who got bad news, folded her tent and went home, she'd asked to speak to the committee. No promises were made, but if she got to meet with them, she planned to be so prepared, they'd have to give her the go-ahead.

Then, if she worked flat out with no interruptions except her day job, she planned to get her dissertation written in record-breaking time. Some people took a couple of years to do it, but this kind of thing came easy to her. She thought she could do it in a couple of months.

In fact, she was counting on that. Until the project was done, her life was on hold—and by life she meant Zack. Two months seemed like a lifetime, but they'd started their relationship fast, and a slowdown might do them good.

She didn't really believe that, but it sounded logical and might help her not miss him so much.

She missed him already. This time last week they'd been at the beach with Bonnie pushing them together as if she thought they were meant to be. Clearing her mind of that memory seemed like a sacrilege, but she had to focus on the work at hand.

Or did she? Was the sacrifice necessary? She didn't want or need a Ph.D. Proving her dad wrong was hardly an incentive, and she hadn't counted on his approval since she'd hit double digits.

She scribbled "Chloe Kilgannon, Ph.D." on a yellow sticky notepad and waited to see if pride would kick in. Would she feel more confident if the moderators of her workshops introduced her as Dr. Kilgannon? She couldn't imagine that she would, and she hated the thought of giving up her life for three letters and a couple of periods.

The only real motivation was her desire for her parents to know the Lord as more than a figure on a cross. If Dad thought she hadn't kept her word, how could he accept her faith as real? How could she pray and not do her part?

Totally absorbed in her thoughts, she didn't notice Cate standing over her with a healthy-looking sandwich and one of her famous fruit drinks.

"Am I invisible or what?" Cate teased. "Here, eat this. I worry about you."

Chloe hadn't realized she was hungry until she saw the food. "Thanks, Cate. You are so good to me. I'd ask you to sit down except—"

"There's no place to sit! Not even the floor. Where are you going to sleep? On the sofa?"

"It doesn't matter. I won't sleep much until my paper is done—if I do it."

"You're not backing out!" Cate's brows drew together in dismay. "Chloe! I stood up for you! I told Dad you'd do that paper and do it fast. I'm making sandwiches for you so you'll get it done."

Chloe hung her head, hearing the truth in Cate's words. "Catie, I'm sorry, but the university has a strict time limit for completing the degree. Over the years I've been in contact with my adviser, but she's no longer there, and my new adviser says I may have to repeat the course work *and* a year of on-campus time. It would mean giving up my job."

"Well, you're not doing that! That's too extreme. Don't worry about it. I don't mind eating my words. No one takes me seriously anyway."

"That's not true. Don't I eat what you say and wear what you say?"

Cate smiled and joy filled the room. She was like that. When Cate was happy, so was everyone else.

"Come join me for a swim," she said. "It will do you good."

"I'd love that, but I'd better stay with my work and keep sorting while I can still remember what's in each stack."

"Okay," Cate said reluctantly, "but if you change your mind…"

"I won't, but thanks anyway." Not only did Chloe have more work to do, Zack had promised to call. She didn't want to miss hearing about his first day back to work. Had he gotten along okay with the Brennans and her dad?

She'd thought he might call when he'd had a break between surgeries or after he'd seen his last patient at the clinic. He might have gone back to the hospital. There could be any number of reasons he hadn't called.

Now that his vacation was over, was this going to be their life? She'd told him she understood the life of a surgeon, and she did…even if she didn't like it.

She went back to sorting data she might never use. Her discontent grew as the stacks of data got higher. She'd set out to find the age when children would give up caution with strangers to accept love from anyone. If she knew that, she might know the approximate age *she* had realized she had to find love from people outside of her home. She'd been a little girl. That was all she remembered.

It was too early for an academic conclusion, but she

knew this: people who had love in their lives—any love at all—had a gold mine of good fortune. For them to complain about the trivialities of life was a shame.

Compared to the lives of children who'd known complete devastation, she shouldn't feel sorry for herself about anything, and Zack shouldn't be so upset just because life had thrown him a curve. It wasn't as if he'd gone without love. Bonnie had been there for him, and now the Brennans wanted to accept him. She herself had supported him while he'd dithered about whether he wanted to be part of the Brennan family. How could he even think of turning down love?

Zack pulled out his cell phone and called Chloe. The family wouldn't question him making a call during a party. It could be patient-related.

His heart raced, wondering what he should say. He felt so bad that she wasn't here on a night he would remember the rest of his life. She wouldn't be as upset as he was, but that didn't make his concern any the less.

When his call went to voice mail, he thought she must have stepped away from her phone. A few minutes later when he tried again and the same thing happened, he realized she might have turned her phone off, the better to concentrate on her project. He should try another number—Carmen's.

She answered right away. "What's up, Zack?"

"Chloe isn't answering her phone, and I told her I'd call."

"So you want me to take my phone to her." There was a smile in her voice.

"Would you? I'll buy your lunch tomorrow."

"Good, since I have to get off my very comfortable chaise and walk all the way into Chloe's bedroom."

He heard her knock on Chloe's door and say, "Zack couldn't get you on your phone. You can use mine."

Chloe took the phone from Carmen and inhaled several deep breaths. It wasn't his fault she was in a bad mood. Everything related to the Ph.D. had thrown her off balance, but he might have had a really bad day. Loving him meant being there for him. She shouldn't have turned off her phone, but waiting for it to ring had made it impossible to concentrate.

She started to apologize for that, but she could hear laughter in the background on his end of the call. "Who's giving the party?" she asked in an upbeat tone that she hoped would hide her dark mood.

He didn't answer, but the party noise continued.

"Hello?" she said. "Anybody there?"

"I'm here."

He didn't sound like himself. His voice was deeper and edged with irritation. Was he annoyed that he'd had to leave a party to fulfill his promise to call? He didn't have to do that on her account.

"Chloe, it's been a big evening for me."

"I can hear that."

"What? Oh, the background noise. Chloe, I'm sorry I forgot to call earlier."

"Think nothing of it. I've been busy organizing my research notes."

"Good. That's good. The noise you hear is coming

from the Brennans. Most of the family are here in Grandpa's office."

"Grandpa?" Zack must have accepted his Brennan family.

"That's what J.T. says I should call him. I met with him late this afternoon, and he persuaded me to let the whole family know I'm Charlie's son."

"That's big!"

"I wish you were here," he said in a wistful tone that made her love him more.

She looked at all the work she had left to do, but was anything more important than sharing a special night with the man she loved? "If you want me there, I can be," she said breathlessly.

"I'd love that."

So would she. "Give me thirty minutes."

"No, it looks like the party's almost over. Most of the people here have to be at the hospital early tomorrow."

"How did Collin take the news? What did Charlie do?"

There was another pause. "Chloe, I'll tell you all about it, but right now everyone's leaving, and I need to say goodbye to them. Okay?"

"Okay," she said uncertainly. Did that mean he would call back later or stop by?

"Goodnight Chloe."

Goodnight? That answered her question. "Zack, if you want to stop by when you're through there, I'll still be up."

"That's okay, Chloe. I have an early-morning surgery, and I should get some sleep. But I'll be thinking of you."

"Then, good night, Zack."

She ended the call before he could tell she was angry.

Was an extra half hour of sleep more important to him than sharing such a big moment of his life? The urge to throw the phone was strong…but it was Carmen's.

She found Carmen on the lanai and put the phone in her hand. "If Zack calls back tonight, I don't want to talk to him. Okay?"

"Lovers' quarrel?" Carmen said, her brows lifted.

"No, but I think I got too serious about him too fast. You wondered about it yourself. I don't think I mean that much to him, Carmen."

"Slowing it down is probably a good idea, but Zack looks like a man in love to me."

"Zack met with his Brennan family tonight. If he were a man in love, wouldn't he have wanted me there?"

"Maybe it was like a surprise party or something."

"J. T. Brennan told Zack to call him Grandpa."

"Well, that's good, isn't it?"

"I don't know. Zack wasn't on the phone long enough to say." Tears welled in her eyes. "Carmen, I honestly don't know why he bothered to call."

"Because he wants you to be part of his life?"

"I would have been with him if he wanted that. I'm beginning to wonder if he just wanted me around to co-host his mother's visit."

"Chloe! Zack's not like that."

"You know him better than I do," Chloe said, barely hiding her sarcasm. How could she have let herself fall for a guy she barely knew? "I think I was just a vacation romance."

"Chloe, are you picking a fight with Zack so you can shut him out and focus on your paper?"

"No!" But she could understand why Carmen might think that. Chloe was good at shutting out the world. Her family thought it was for greater academic concentration. More often it had been to avoid the reality of her parents' preference for her sisters.

To prove Carmen wrong, she said, "There may not be a paper. I may not get my doctorate degree."

"What!"

Chloe told Carmen the variables of getting the degree. Like Cate, Carmen urged her to forget about it. Chloe knew it was excellent advice, but to keep her word to her dad, she would work on it until all doors slammed in her face.

Back in her room, she stared at the mirror over the vanity that doubled as her desk. "You're a fraud," she whispered to the woman in the mirror.

The image looked too lost to argue.

"You said that people who had love in their lives had nothing to complain about, yet you're falling apart over a couple of disappointments. What's wrong with you?"

The woman wouldn't say, but a tear slipped down her cheek.

"You have sisters who love you. There are always children to love. Even if you are wrong about Zack's feelings for you, you have nothing to complain about."

The woman in the mirror closed her eyes and shut Chloe out.

Fine. She should be talking with the Lord anyway.

Zack was the last to leave the party, and his was the last car in the parking lot. He should be bone tired, but he was as wired as a kid high on birthday sweets. Would he sleep at all tonight?

Before he drove out of the lot, he admired the dramatic shading of lights on the building. To think that one day he would be in charge of this place was unbelievable! There would be others to guide him, but Grandpa was counting on him.

Grandpa—how awesome that he could think of the chief that way. Maybe it came from hearing it said so many times tonight, but saying it put Zack right in the middle of unconditional love.

Two weeks ago…not even that…eleven days ago, he'd met Mom's plane and anticipated showing his mom a great time—nothing more. He hadn't known he was a Brennan, he hadn't known Chloe and he hadn't known how much his life would change.

He drove toward his condo, thinking that his amazing day seemed like a fantasy. He was the future CEO of a billion-dollar clinic. The responsibility of it boggled his mind. Recognition and power could go to a man's head…if he hadn't been raised by Roland Hemingway. Chloe would say Roland's influence was part of God's plan. Tonight Zack was willing to believe it might be.

At least it was something to think about, but Chloe herself ranked number one on his mind. She hadn't sounded like herself tonight. He might have been late in making the call, but he *had* called, and he'd had the best reason in the world for being late.

It wasn't like she'd been sitting around waiting for him to call. She was busy with her research. She sounded so happy for him that the Brennan secret was out, but by the time their call had ended, her tone had changed.

Was Chloe upset with him? Nothing bothered him more than feeling he'd let someone down, especially someone he loved.

Her house wasn't much out of his way. She said she'd still be up. How could he sleep without checking on his girl?

There seemed to be lights in every room at Carmen's house, and the pool area was lit, too. He rang the doorbell and Carmen answered. From the damp robe she wore and her wet hair, it was a safe guess she'd been swimming.

"Have you come for a swim?" she said, toweling her hair.

"No, I was just passing by." It was an old line, but Carmen wouldn't mind. "The truth is, I want to talk to Chloe, and I thought she might not take my call."

"Good guess. What did you do to make her think she was your vacation romance?"

That was a jab to his heart. "She thinks that? Why?"

"Spoken just like a man. Cross the line and then say you didn't see it. It takes a lot for Chloe to think negatively, but she's there."

"I've got to talk to her."

"She just got into the pool. May I suggest that you wait a few minutes to let her work out some of her anger?"

He'd always thought the measure of a person was what made them mad. What had he done to upset Chloe?

"Make yourself comfortable on the lanai. Take off your shoes and put up your feet. Can I get you a soda or something?"

"I'm fine."

On the dark lanai, Zack rolled up his sleeves, slipped off his shoes and socks and stretched out on the sofa. He would have enjoyed watching Chloe swim, but he closed his eyes and just listened.

The noisy splashes from her kicks sounded as if she were racing for the gold, but little by little the churning sound died. Water still lapped the pool edge, so she must be floating...and crying. That was definitely a sob he heard.

The thought of Chloe crying was a knife in his heart. He was off the sofa and moving toward her as if he were needed for a code blue. "Chloe, honey, swim over here to me."

Startled, she looked up at him with horror and sank under the water.

But she'd have to come up.

Or not.

She was under so long that fear kicked in. He did a shallow dive to look for her. Where was she? Not where she'd gone down.

He surfaced, gasping for air, and saw her at the deep end of the pool, treading water. She was not happy to see him, and he was soaking wet in his street clothes.

Chapter Eighteen

"What are you doing here?" she asked bluntly to cover her embarrassment.

"Right now, I'm wondering that myself."

"How long were you watching me?"

"I didn't *watch* you. I was waiting for you on the lanai. I heard you crying."

"I wasn't crying." That was a lie. What had she come to that she would lie to keep her pride?

"I couldn't stand to think you were sad."

She started to say she wasn't sad, but that would have been another lie. She *wasn't* sad now, not if he cared about her. He'd ruined his suit pants, and she had an idea what they cost.

"Chloe, we need to talk but I'd rather not share with the neighbors. Will you stay put long enough for me to swim to you?"

"Wouldn't you rather get out of the pool?"

"Not yet." He swam toward her slowly, smoothly, barely making a ripple.

"Do you have your shoes on?" She wondered if he'd ruined those, too.

"Nope. No socks either. How about you?"

He was so close he could probably see for himself. The borrowed swimsuit belonged to Carmen, and it was red, Carmen's favorite color.

He swam to the side. "Come over here," he invited, holding on to the edge of the pool.

If they were going to talk, she'd rather not tread water. She swam to the side, but kept a few feet between them.

His eyes moved across her face as if he were worried about her. They lingered on her mouth, and she felt the familiar tingles of attraction. It would be nice if they had a shut-off switch she could control.

"You're not smiling," he said, his brows knit together with concern. "In my mind, you're always smiling. Tell me what's wrong, Chloe."

She started to say that nothing was wrong, but the worried look on his face got past her defenses. "It was a combination of things," she said cautiously, unwilling to make herself unnecessarily vulnerable.

He came to her and gently turned her face to him. "Did I hurt you, Chloe?"

She looked away. She didn't want to lie again, and she didn't want to cry.

"I did!" The anguish in his words went straight to her heart. When he reached to draw her closer, she didn't resist.

"This might have been the biggest day of my life," he said reflectively, "but driving home, all I could think of was you and how much I wanted to see you."

And she'd been thinking they might be over. She *never* wanted it to be over. She put both arms on his shoulders, trusting him to keep them afloat as he held onto the edge with one hand.

With his free hand, he pulled her closer. "It's amazing, this feeling I have when I'm with you."

"I know," she admitted. This closeness, this sense of belonging, this yearning never to let him go—it was precious beyond words.

"Don't give up on me, Chloe."

"I won't." It was a huge promise, but her feelings for him were that strong.

"My life is going to get even busier, but you have to know I want to share it with you. Grandpa says he expects *me* to head BMC's board of directors when he steps down. Isn't that incredible?"

"Not really." She ran her finger across his face slowly, loving the right to show him she cared. "You're an exceptional man, Zack Hemingway."

The love in her eyes just knocked him out. What would it be like to have a woman like Chloe for his wife?

A woman *like* Chloe?

Had he avoided the thought of marriage so long he couldn't name this wonderful woman? Maybe they hadn't known each other long enough to test their love or examine every little thing, but didn't they have the rest of their lives for that?

"Chloe," he said, so afraid she would turn him down, "can you see yourself ever wanting to marry me?"

"Is that sort of a test proposal?" Her eyes seemed to laugh at him, but she hadn't turned him down.

"I guess so, but you'd be crazy to say yes."

"And why would that be?" she teased.

When he'd made the remark, it was just a silly disclaimer—a way of saying he knew he wasn't perfect. But now that it was out there, the remark could serve another purpose as well. He wanted her to know what she was getting into. He'd seen so many of his colleagues' marriages fail.

"Chloe, better than most women, you know what a surgeon's life is like. You'd have to be a little bit crazy to marry me, knowing how little time I would have for you. You saw your mother's life."

"Mom went solo plenty of times, but don't tell her she was crazy to marry Dad! She's proud to be his wife."

"But you're not your mother, Chloe."

"Thank you for that," she said with a grin. "I am nothing like her, so why are we talking about her?"

"I guess I wanted to point out that she's from a different generation. She didn't mind taking second place to Sterling's work, but I would think you would mind a lot."

"I would be taking second place to your work?" She pushed away and did a slow rotation in the water as if she were digesting that thought.

Had he been wrong to bring up the subject? Surgery was his life. It had always come first. He didn't want to mislead her.

"You know, you were right to offer me a test proposal," she said, treading water. "Since it was only a test, you can pretend you didn't mention marriage, and I'll pretend you didn't offer me second place in your life."

"I don't think you're taking this like I meant it."

"Oh, I think I got it. You're a great catch, Zack. You won't have any trouble finding women who'll be glad to be second, third…pick a number…*any* place as long as they get Dr. Zack Hemingway, future CEO of Brennan Medical Clinic."

He'd wondered what it would take to make her angry. This was it, but he'd dealt with enough high emotion for one day and couldn't find a way to regroup.

"I've never been first in anyone's life," she said, her face a mixture of hurt and pride. "I guess second place is a step up, but I'll pass on that honor. The man I marry—*if* I ever do—may not be able to spend as much time with me as I would like. Lots of couples experience that, Zack, and they're not even *surgeons.*"

He could have done without the sarcasm.

"If I marry, I'll love my guy so much he'll never doubt where he stands in my heart, and he won't think of me as—"

She pressed her lips together and looked as if she were going to cry, but she dove under the water.

He didn't look to see where she came up. He heard her pull herself out of the water and pad across the deck. It would break his heart if the last image of the woman he loved was her running from him.

Zack drove home with a beach towel wrapped around his waist. Carmen had taken pity on him and put his wet clothes in a bag. They hadn't talked. He couldn't have without losing it.

While he got ready for bed, he replayed the day, beginning with the part where the chief had said to call him Grandpa and ending with Chloe saying she would pass on the honor of being his wife.

He'd really messed up, but he sure hadn't intended to.

It was just that he'd seen the marriages of other doctors. Some wives were appeased with the material things a Beverly Hills doctor could provide. Some understood the priority of their men taking care of people in pain, and others went looking for something better, taking the man's kids and half his assets.

He'd asked Chloe not to give up on him. She'd promised she wouldn't, but then he'd foolishly talked about second place—a term he would never use again!

What if he hadn't come straight from the biggest stress of his life? What if she'd been there to share it with him? And what if she hadn't felt the pressure of writing her dissertation?

If he stayed out of her life while she wrote her paper, would she give him another chance? Could he stay out of her life?

It might be simpler just to forget about Chloe.

But that was like saying, forget how to breathe.

Two months later

It was the Fourth of July, and Chloe and her sisters celebrated while her dissertation printed out. They lay on her bed and sang what they could remember of patriotic tunes. When they came to the words *free* and *freedom*, they belted them out loud enough for the neighbors to hear.

As the last pages were done, Chloe handed them

over to Cate, who put them in a red, white and blue box, and Carmen stood by, ready to attach a snazzy blue bow with fake firecrackers. Cate had sung the loudest, though slightly off-key; Carmen had seemed to take forever, getting the bow just right, and Chloe had never loved her sisters more.

If it hadn't been for them, she might not have been so persistent with the faculty committee, and if it hadn't been for their support, she couldn't have gotten the project done in two months. Today at Albert and Amy Brennan's annual Fourth of July party, they planned to make a production of presenting the dissertation to their dad, marking Chloe's freedom. They wanted no more accusations that Chloe didn't keep her word and didn't meet her obligations.

Carmen hadn't been able to avoid seeing their father since she worked with him, but neither Carmen nor Cate had spent social time with Dad or Mom. Her sisters said they were through looking the other way. They'd made a pact to continue the standoff until their parents appreciated Chloe as they should.

Chloe felt the burden of that and would do anything to bring her sisters and her parents back together. "Anything" included making the presentation at the party where Zack was almost sure to be. Would he talk to her? Would she think of the right thing to say?

"I'm going to be so mad if Dad doesn't get the symbolism of this gift on this holiday," Cate said, plunking herself back down on Chloe's bed. "Do we all know our lines?"

"We're going to look silly, but I'm ready," Chloe said.

"I'm counting on us looking silly," Carmen claimed.

"If we don't leave Dad a way to save face, this is not going to work."

"We could still messenger the gift with a note that says our lines," Chloe said. She hated confrontation with a passion.

"Nope. We're going," Carmen said firmly, putting the box on Chloe's desk. "We go to Albert and Amy's every year, and we always have fun."

"But it is going to be awkward this year," Cate argued. "Mom's mad at me because I'm mad at Dad. Chloe hasn't spoken to Zack in two months."

"Do you think he'll be there?" Chloe asked, wishing she didn't have to know.

"That's funny. He asked the same thing about you," Carmen teased.

"He did not." She didn't really doubt Carmen. It was just such a relief to hear that Zack might be thinking of her.

"Zack asks about you all the time," Carmen said, joining Cate on the bed. "'How's her dissertation going, Carmen?' 'Is Chloe getting enough rest?' 'Did Chloe enjoy her conference in Seattle?' 'Did she like Chicago?' I think he gets your conference schedule off the Internet."

"You're making this up," Chloe said flatly.

"No, she's not," Cate said. "When Zack trains with me, he digs for information all the time."

"What do you tell him?"

"That you're working hard on your paper. What else is there to say? Die-hard hermits get out more than you do. By the way, since we're talking about him, does this mean that your ban on all-things-Zack is over?"

"I guess it is. I'm sorry to be such a crank about it, but whenever I thought about him, I'd lose all concentration and couldn't get back to work for hours. That, of course, was not good for getting my work done—"

"And we *did* want that paper done!" Cate said earnestly.

"Yes, we did!" Chloe agreed.

Looking back at that night in the pool, she knew she may have overreacted to his second-place comment. She'd treated him like a self-centered, arrogant jerk, which he wasn't at all. That night had been more about her own fear than anything he'd said. She'd begun to think she couldn't live without him, and that had scared her to death.

"I have a confession," Carmen said. "Do you remember when I asked if you and Zack weren't falling for each other too fast?"

"Of course. We'd wondered about it ourselves."

"While I still think it's best to get to know each other over a long period of time, I believe that what you and Zack have is the real thing."

Chloe's heart seemed to skip a beat. "What made you change your mind?"

"Well, Zack's sitting on top of the world these days. Not only is he the top orthopedist on the West Coast, one of these days, he'll head Brennan Medical Clinic. The word's out on that, and even Dad treats him with extra respect. And how is Zack reacting to all this good fortune? Like a guy who's lost the love of his life."

"Okay, as long as we're allowed to talk about Zack," Cate said, "I'm going to tell you that I'm really worried about him. He's training too hard, and he's not taking in enough calories. When you see him this afternoon, Chloe, don't be surprised that he's become all muscle and bone."

"Isn't that supposed to be good?" Chloe asked.

Cate looked at Carmen. "What do you think?"

Carmen sighed. "She'll have to see for herself."

While Zack shaved, he prayed about how things would go today. He'd never been the guest of honor at any event, but that was what Albert and Amy said he was for their big party of the year. The guest list went beyond the inner circle of Cedar Hills' medical community and would include most of their colleagues and families. The plan was that after dinner, Grandpa would tell everyone that Zack was a Brennan.

Zack trusted Grandpa to keep the embarrassment factor down, but there was no getting around the fact that Zack was Charlie's unrecognized son, and most of the guests would be learning it for the first time. It might have been less stressful if the hospital rumor mill had picked up on it, but the Brennans had been discreet. If anyone knew it outside of the family, Zack wasn't aware of it.

Carmen and Chloe knew, but they were like family and he'd given Carmen permission to tell Cate. Carmen said the three of them planned to make a big deal of presenting their father with a copy of Chloe's dissertation.

She'd gotten it done—which blew Zack's mind. He'd never heard of anyone completing the process so quickly, but she was a brilliant woman with a beautiful spirit and a great big heart.

I'll love my guy so much he'll never doubt where he stands.

That was what she'd said that awful night. He hadn't forgotten. How could he forget when the sentence had looped in his mind every day for two months? He'd wondered what it would feel like to be loved like that. When he saw her today, one look into her chocolate-brown eyes and he'd know if he had another chance.

She wasn't the kind of woman who would play games and pretend one thing when she felt another. If she loved him, he would know it.

Dear Lord, it's me again with the same prayer. Let Chloe know how much I love her. Let her trust me, Lord. I know You provide even more than we ask for—more than we can dream of. I know it's all contingent upon it being Your will. If you have a better man planned for Chloe, so be it. But I can't see how there could be anyone better than Chloe for me.

Chapter Nineteen

At Amy and Albert Brennan's house, it truly was the Fourth of July. An enormous American flag whipped in the breeze overhead, and it was red, white and blue everywhere beneath—in the bunting at the foot of the stage in the big white tent, along the flag-lined driveway and even sprayed onto the hair of the valet parking attendants.

A band and a DJ would take turns on stage. Right now, the DJ was in charge, and patriotic march tunes set a lively mood.

Wearing a dazzling red, white and blue top hat, Albert greeted his guests. Amy welcomed newcomers in the backyard where the huge white tent provided shade. Zack's self-appointed job was to greet the kids.

If he were ever to have a life with Chloe, he'd concluded that he had to learn to appreciate kids. His cousin, pediatrician Beth Brennan-McKnight, had given him a crash course. The first lesson had been that his interest had to be genuine. To practice "keeping it real," he'd turned to his little second cousins and learned that a man missed a lot without kids in his life.

Kids loved presents, and Zack had come to the party prepared. He had stars-and-stripes scrunchies, baseball hats, shoelaces, bandannas and yo-yos. A kid didn't get a present without giving him a hug or a cool handshake. Collin had briefed him on those.

His nurse, Marsha, had just arrived with her grandchildren, and he was helping the kids make a choice when suddenly he felt the presence of someone behind him.

He looked up, and it was Chloe! She smiled at him, and he wondered how he'd lived without that smile in his life. Her beautiful hair was held back by a red, white and blue sun visor, and she wore a white outfit that made her look as if she belonged in his arms.

"What are you doing, Zack?" she said, her eyes skimming his face as if she were so glad to see him.

"Making new friends," he answered, loving her more than she could possibly know.

"Good for you!"

That bit of praise made his heart swell.

"Hi, Zack," Carmen and Cate said almost at the same time.

Carmen reached out for a hug. Cate did, too.

Chloe could see why her sisters were worried about Zack. The muscles he'd put on were a body builder's dream, and strangers would think he looked great in his white shorts and white polo shirt with stars-and-stripes trim, but people who really knew him would be concerned about the gaunt look in his face. Was he that worried about being revealed as a Brennan today?

He glanced at her, as if he'd like to hug her, too, but wasn't sure if she'd want that. The uncertain look on his face tugged at her heart, and she went for the hug, hoping it was the right thing.

The way he held on to her said it definitely was.

"I'm looking for the Kilgannon sisters," a man dressed as Uncle Sam said.

"Who is he?" Chloe whispered.

"The party planner," Zack whispered back.

"We're the Kilgannons," Cate said with Carmen beside her.

"You'd better join them," Zack whispered.

"Okay." It was so good to be talking to Zack again.

Uncle Sam said, "We're kicking off the party with your presentation. Dr. Brennan! Dr. Brennan! Oh, somebody, get the man's attention."

"I'm here, Sam," Albert said, hustling over to them.

"If you want to see the Kilgannon presentation, it's time you joined your wife. One of my people will take your post."

Albert nodded and walked briskly to the tent.

"Are our parents here?" Carmen asked.

"They are," Zack answered. "They were seated at a table where they'd have a clear view."

"Who are you?" Sam asked rudely.

"Someone you want to be nicer to," Cate sassed. "He's the guest of honor."

Sam checked his clipboard. "Ah, Dr. Hemingway. If you want to see the presentation, follow Dr. Brennan now."

"I'll be waiting for you there," Zack said in Chloe's ear.

"Line up, ladies," Sam ordered. "Three abreast. Tall

girl in the middle. Where's the box? There's supposed to be a box."

Chloe lifted it high for him to see. This guy was too much.

"Okay, ladies. Listen for the fanfare. March to the cadence. Left foot first." And he was off to boss somebody else.

"Do you see Mom and Dad?" Cate asked.

"Like Zack said, straight ahead," Carmen answered.

Chloe took a deep breath. "I can't believe we're really going to do this."

"Well, we are," Carmen said fiercely. "Heads up, shoulders back. We're women with a mission."

A brass trio stood and blasted out an impressive fanfare. The drummer set a fancy cadence, and Chloe and her sisters marched across the lawn toward their parents.

Chloe hadn't imagined their presentation would be this formal, but it appealed to her sense of humor. It was all she could do not to laugh, especially when their father realized they were bearing down on him and he was to be the center of attention. The drummer brought them to a halt in front of him. Mom stood beside him, surprised delight on her face.

"Well, hello, girls. You're looking very patriotic," he said.

Carmen had the first line, and she began, "Dad, we have a gift we'd like to present. The Fourth of July celebrates freedom. It's the perfect day for Chloe to present you with her completed doctoral dissertation."

Chloe tried not to smile as she presented the box as if it were gold. "And with that done," she said formally,

"I hereby declare my *freedom* from the claim that I don't keep my word!"

"So there you go, Dad," Cate said, breaking the formality. "Read it or burn it. It's done, and Chloe did it for you."

Chloe held her breath, waiting for his usual deprecating remarks, but he stood and lifted the box over his head like an athlete holding a trophy. "Did you hear that, everybody? There's a new doctor in the family! Let's hear it for Dr. Chloe Kilgannon!"

It was a premature announcement. Chloe still had to defend her dissertation before the doctoral committee, but she enjoyed seeing her dad in good humor. Even her mother seemed pleased. Mom hugged her and said, "Good girl, Chloe."

At twenty-eight, she wasn't a girl, but she might have been one the last time Mom had bragged on her. She wouldn't complain when she had the opportunity to put her arms around her mother.

After Mom's hug came Dad's—a little impersonal, but a hug nonetheless. Even better, he said, "I'm proud of you, Chloe."

She could live on that for a long time.

There were lots of hugs from friends, including all of the Brennans. But not Zack. Where did he go?

Collin gave Chloe a kiss on the cheek and whispered, "He's been lost without you, hon. I'm glad that paper is done."

Is that what they all thought? That she and Zack hadn't been seeing each other because she'd been working on her paper? Zack hadn't told them how awful she'd been?

And then Zack was standing beside her. "Can we go somewhere and talk?" he asked softly.

She nodded. She had a big apology to make.

He took her hand and headed toward the house as Albert's voice came over the sound system, inviting the guests to eat.

"Are you hungry?" Zack asked. "Would you like to…"

"I'd rather talk, but if you'd…"

He shook his head and walked toward the house. When they were in his uncle's den and the door was closed to the hall, she got right to it. "Zack, I want to apologize for—"

He put a finger over her lips. "The fault was all mine. What we had was so new…I didn't handle things right…I didn't know…" He stopped and rubbed the back of his neck. "I've practiced this for two months and still can't get it right, but it comes down to this. I love you, Chloe. I love you more than I knew I could love anyone."

Chloe reached up and circled his neck. She laid her head on his shoulder and closed her eyes. He nestled his face against her hair. This was where she belonged, and nothing was better than being here in his arms. He cupped her head and touched her lips lightly with his.

He stroked her hair as if she were precious to him. "I think I've figured out why I was so callous that awful night in the pool, talking about first place and second—"

"We don't need to talk about that," she interrupted.

"That was my fault. I loved you, and I was afraid of losing you."

"But, see, honey, that was it. You already knew how to love. You've loved thousands of children. Who have I loved in life? Just my mom. When you said that you could love a guy so much he'd never have to wonder where he stood, I didn't comprehend that kind of love."

"You remembered what I said?"

"Only every day—morning, noon and night. I didn't know what it was like to need a hug, a kiss, the touch of one person so much that I thought I would die without it. I thought my work was my life, but I found out I can barely *do* my work if you're not in my life."

They looked into each other's eyes. She touched his cheek to prove this was real. He caressed her face and planted little kisses here and there. She loved every one.

"Chloe, we may never have as much time to be together as we would like, but the time we do have…I want to share with you."

Her eyes opened wide. "Is this another test proposal?"

"I don't want it to be." He grinned for the first time today. "Chloe Kilgannon, would you be my bride?"

"Yes! No! Zack, there's one thing I have to tell you. I should have before now, but the first day it was appropriate, you were caught up in the news that you were a Brennan. I just couldn't give you anything to worry about."

He didn't speak for a second. It seemed like forever. "Chloe, could you please assure me that you're not backing out?"

"No, I'm not backing out, but you might want to. I've

got to give you that chance. What I have to say might change your mind about wanting to marry me."

"Chloe! Nothing could change my mind about that!"

She took his hand. "I've still got to tell you."

"Okay. Go ahead." He looked at her with such love and confidence, she wished she could skip the whole thing, but it had to be said.

"I can't have children," she said bluntly. "That's why I mentioned adopting. My appendix ruptured when I was out of the country, and decent medical care wasn't available. As a doctor, you can probably guess what happened. And before you ask, I had second and third opinions that confirmed the worst."

He tenderly stroked her face. "I'm sorry, honey. That must be so hard for you. I can't even imagine how hard."

She didn't want to cry, but he was just so sweet. "Zack, I've had two years to get used to the fact that I'll never hold a little baby just born from my body. Once you've had a chance to absorb it, you may realize that having children of your own—"

"Don't go there, Chloe. Please, don't go there."

"But your mom said—"

"You know Mom better than that! What would she want for me—a child with my DNA or the woman I love?"

"I know she would want you to be happy."

"How could I be happy without you? And I'm the last guy who's going to care about passing on his DNA."

"Are you saying you don't want to have children, Zack?" She couldn't help the tremor in her voice.

He reached for her hand. "Chloe, didn't you see me playing with the kids at the party? I'm playing catch-up on learning to love kids, and I'm playing catch-up on reading the Word and learning to trust God. The Lord knows what he wants *for* us...and *from* us. Whatever it is, we're going to do it. Right?"

She nodded, overwhelmed that he'd thought ahead and worked on the two issues that could have kept them apart.

"The first day I saw you, I heard you talk about the kids out there with no one to love them. I got the message. With your help, I'm ready to step up. When God shows us which children He wants us to raise, they'll be our sons and daughters. And they'll never question where they stand in our hearts. Okay?"

"Okay," she said, tears brimming over. It was perfect, in fact. "I love you so much."

"Good! Are you going to marry me?"

"Yes! Do we have the Elvis wedding chapel booked?"

"No, but it can be arranged." He picked her up and twirled her around.

"We're really engaged?" she asked, wondering how she could go from lonely to happily-ever-after in one afternoon.

"It's official!" he exclaimed. "And tomorrow we'll go shopping for a ring."

"But it's not official without a ring."

Zack's heart seemed to stop. She couldn't mean that.

"Fortunately, I have one." She pulled a long gold chain from beneath her shirt. Hanging from it was the big fake diamond ring that Flower had offered him not so long ago. "Will this do for now?"

"How did you know we were going to need this?" He was astonished that she had it with her.

"I didn't know. I carry it with me all the time. I love to remember the day I 'fell' for you."

He'd never thought of himself as a sentimental guy, but that did him in. He held her, wondering how he'd ever not loved this woman.

Eventually he took the ring and, as Flower had done, dropped to one knee, extending the ring toward her. "This is no test proposal, Chloe. It's as real as it can be…with a clown ring. Will you marry me?"

"Yes! *Now* it's official."

He kissed the ring and put the chain on her again before scooping her up in his arms. "Who do you want to tell first?"

"It's got to be your mom."

He grinned, pulled out his cell phone and put it on speaker so both of them could hear her reaction.

She had caller ID, so she answered, "Zack? Happy Fourth of July!"

"Oh, Mom, you have no idea how happy it is. Guess who I have with me."

"Well, since this is the first time in two months that you sound like yourself, I would guess Chloe. Is she there with you?"

"I am," Chloe said, "and I'm a happily engaged woman."

There was a tap at the door, and Collin stuck his head in. "Grandpa's ready to make the announcement, Zack."

"We'll be right there."

Chloe was glad Bonnie wasn't here to see the instant tension in Zack's eyes.

"Mom, we've got to go. It's pretty hectic here. There's a rumor that Charlie intends to take the mike."

"Then I'd better pray for you. Congratulations, my darlings."

Zack held Chloe's hand as they hurried across the lawn to the front of the tent. On the stage, J. T. Brennan sat in a wheelchair. Albert stood beside him, and the rest of the Brennans stood at ground level in front of them. They made a space for Zack and Chloe in the middle by Collin and his wife.

"I don't belong here," she whispered in protest.

"And I do?" he whispered back. "Chloe, you're my family more than they are. You don't have to stand beside me if you don't want to, but it would mean a lot to me if you did."

Then of course she would stay.

Collin's wife, Glenda, linked arms with Chloe and whispered, "We'll get through this together."

"We will," Chloe whispered back. This had to be hard on Glenda and Collin, too. "Where's Charlie?"

"The party planner told him there was a woman who wanted to meet him. I think it's a distraction to keep Charlie busy until this is over."

It was a good plan. Chloe had to give Uncle Sam his due. He really did take care of the details of a party.

"Friends," J.T. began soberly, "every year we take advantage of Albert and Amy's fine hospitality to celebrate the freedom of our great nation. Today, the Brennan family claims the 'freedom' to openly say we have a new addition to the Brennan family."

He paused when the family applauded and made too

much noise for him to go on. Zack had a family united behind him.

Zack leaned over and whispered in her ear, "I won't be the newest addition for long. You'll have the title, honey."

"That's right. Enjoy it while you can," she teased.

J.T. began again. "This new member *was* a Brennan for thirty-one years without knowing he belonged to us. We deeply regret that, but we're very grateful we can claim him now. It is time, *past* time, that all of you know that Zack Hemingway is not only a fine doctor, he's my grandson."

The audience reacted with open-mouthed wonder and then quick applause. Surprised chatter passed through the crowd like a breeze.

That was fine with Zack. He turned to Chloe, "I think that went well."

"I peeked at you and Collin. You both did great."

Zack felt himself being shoved out of the way.

It was Charlie trying to work his way up to the stage. "C'mon, boys, this is our day. I want to get up there and tell everybody that you're both mine."

"Not today, Dad," Collin said, putting his body in the way.

Zack wasn't about to let his brother do all the work. He added his muscle to keep Charlie in line.

Charlie's older brother James yanked Charlie back by his sleeve. "Can't you think about someone besides yourself for once?"

Without remorse or penance, Charlie grinned from ear to ear. "But both of these fine boys are mine. I've never been prouder."

There might come a day when Zack would be interested in what Charlie had to say, but this wasn't it. The exhilarating joy of knowing Chloe loved him filled his heart and left no room for any regrets.

While Charlie was shuffled out of the way, Collin and Chloe's sisters crowded beside them. Sterling and Ava were there with the rest of this family. "Shall we tell them about us?" Zack whispered to Chloe.

Chloe nodded, loving the happy look on his face.

He took her in his arms and kissed her before shouting out, "Hey everybody, we're engaged!"

Over the cheers and applause, Collin shouted, "Where's the ring?"

"We're getting it tomorrow."

"Make it a big one," Collin joked. "Show her how much you care."

"When's the wedding day?" someone else asked.

"Soon," Chloe answered, getting a laugh. She didn't want a big ring or a big wedding. She just wanted to be Zack's wife.

Chapter Twenty

Fine Diamonds by Orlando Stuart. That was the sign on the Rodeo Drive jewelry store Zack had taken her to.

"Zack, think of the starving children in the world. We don't have to shop at such an expensive place."

He bent down to kiss her. "Orlando Stuart is a patient, honey. I've replaced both of his knees. He'd be very hurt if we went anywhere else, and I expect he'll give us a good price."

The store was understated elegance in gold, silver and black, and their elegant saleswoman was a chic blonde wearing chic black. Chloe might have been in awe of both the store and the woman at one time, but she felt confident with Zack by her side.

Zack asked if Orlando was in the store, and a middle-aged man in a classic double-breasted suit rose from a seat behind the back counter. He had a full head of black hair, a deep tan and a magnetic smile that showed off very white teeth.

"Dr. Hemingway! How nice to see you. Are we buying diamonds for this beautiful woman today?"

Zack smiled down at her. "We are. An engagement ring and wedding bands for us both. This is my fiancée, Chloe Kilgannon."

Orlando must have met thousands of brides-to-be, but he made Chloe feel as if she were the first. He asked if she knew what she wanted and didn't act as if she were a ditz for not knowing.

Her fingers were slender, and all of the rings were too big. Orlando measured her finger and tried to describe how the ring would look on her hand. She knew she liked solitaires best, but even among them, there were too many cuts and carat sizes to choose from.

Zack had been patient, but she could tell he wished she would make a decision. She couldn't. It just wasn't in her to say she wanted a ring that cost this much money. "Zack, please choose for me. I'll go for a walk down the block. Call me when you're done."

He frowned. "Are you sure? You'll be the one wearing that ring the next fifty years or so."

"I'm sure," she said, grinning as she walked out the door.

"Dr. Hemingway," Orlando said, "if it would help your decision-making, I can tell you that many of your colleagues upgrade their wives' rings long before fifty years."

"I know, and others upgrade their wives."

"I didn't want to say that, but—" Orlando shrugged.

"My fiancée would be more likely to sell her ring to feed the poor than allow me to upgrade it."

"A generous woman with a big heart?"

"Very."

"You are a blessed man, Doctor. What would you like for your Chloe to wear?"

It was a difficult decision, but Zack knew his girl. She'd liked the solitaires, especially one brilliant cut diamond Orlando had insisted she try. She'd taken it off fast and said, "It's too much." But he'd liked the look of it on her hand. That was the one.

There was a goldsmith on the premises who could size the ring in an hour. While he waited, he looked at wedding rings, and with Orlando's guidance, chose a platinum band for Chloe and a similar one for himself.

When Chloe's engagement ring was ready, he gave her a call. They met at his car.

She laughed when she saw the gift bag, clapped her hands and said, "Can I see it?"

"When we're in the car," he teased, anticipating her surprise.

In the car, he put the gift bag on the seat between them and put the keys in the ignition, as if he planned to drive away.

"Hey!" Chloe protested. "You said, 'when we get to the car.' We're in the car!"

"Yeah, but this isn't a very romantic setting. We ought to go to a more memorable place."

She pulled out her neck chain and dangled the clown diamond ring before him. "If I can keep a memory like this close to my heart, what do I care about a memorable place?"

"We could make a trade? Flower's diamond for the one in the bag, sight unseen."

"Let me think about it." She let all of two seconds pass. "Okay, it's a deal."

He opened the bag, produced the box with her diamond and popped the lid.

Her open-mouthed gasp seemed to go on forever. She stared at it as if she couldn't believe this was her ring. When she caught her breath, he thought she would say something, but she caught another breath and yet another.

"Zack, I can barely speak. It's the most beautiful ring I've ever seen." She stuck out her left hand and looked at him with anticipation.

He placed the ring on her finger and sealed it in place with a kiss.

"Zack?"

"Yes, honey?"

"Do you know how much I love you?"

He thought so. He hoped so. But he wasn't a guy who took love for granted.

"You fill up my heart." She put her hand on her chest. "Right here. Remember that. It's more than wanting to be with you and thinking about you when I'm not. It's wanting our dreams combined into one life, and it's wanting your good before my own. Do you understand?"

He nodded. He was too moved to speak.

"No matter how busy we become, no matter how little time we have for each other, you have all the love there is in this life. I'll always be loving you more than you'll know."

If Zack hadn't been beside her, Chloe wouldn't have had the courage to be sitting by her parents' pool. She and Zack had come as a courtesy to talk about their wedding. The last time she was here, she'd left feeling shamed and embarrassed. How would she feel leaving here tonight?

Neither she nor Zack wanted a big wedding or a long engagement, but they felt sure her parents would try to talk them into both. Being on the defensive was not a nice way to start a conversation, and she'd asked the Lord to bring them through this smoothly.

"Honey, it's going to be okay," Zack said, picking up on her stress. He seemed really good at that. "We know what we want, and we'll just stick to it."

She leaned toward him, and he met her with a sweet kiss. It had been that way with them since their engagement.

"Here we are," her dad said, setting down a tray with a pitcher of iced tea and a plate of cookies. He poured their tea while her mother settled herself in the chair beside Zack.

"Chloe, I have good news," her mother began excitedly. "I have a dressmaker who can make you a marvelous gown, and I've talked to the best wedding planner in L.A. You two are going to have the wedding of the year."

Zack cleared his throat. "Thank you, Ava. It's just like you to be so thoughtful."

That was so diplomatic Chloe wanted to hug him.

"Chloe and I have looked at our calendars for a wedding date," Zack continued. "We had to find a weekend when she isn't booked for an out-of-town conference, and we need a week after the wedding when I can get away. Grandpa wants to give us a honeymoon in Hawaii like he and Grandma had."

"So are you thinking this time next year or the year after that?" Ava asked. "To reserve the church and the country club at the date you want, you sometimes have to wait."

Chloe bit her lip and looked at Zack, wondering how he would diplomatically answer that.

"The date we've chosen is the second weekend in September."

Sterling nodded. "A year and two months. That should work, shouldn't it, Ava?"

"Excuse me, Sterling," Zack said firmly. "Chloe and I are going to be married this September, not a year from now."

"Impossible!" Ava protested. "No one puts together a wedding in two months."

"They have these destination weddings, Mom," Chloe said tentatively. "Zack and I can get married in Hawaii and avoid all the fuss. The family can join us. We just want something simple."

Tears rolled down Ava's cheeks. "My first daughter getting married, and she doesn't need me. Sterling, do something."

He patted his wife's hand. "Why not get married here at the house?" he suggested. "It could take the place of one of our Sunday night suppers."

Zack looked at Chloe; she looked back. Silently, they agreed. It could work.

"The friends and family we'd like to have at our wedding *are* your regular Sunday night guests," Zack said. "Ava, could you plan a very simple wedding for us at short notice?"

She sniffed. "Of course I can. I may enlist a little help, but I do that every week. It won't be the wedding of the year, but Chloe can walk down our marvelous staircase."

"We bought the house for that staircase," Sterling joked. "All the girls used to pretend they were brides, walking down the stairs with their bathrobes trailing behind them."

Chloe remembered that. She'd never had a boy-friend, but she'd loved the idea of being a bride. Dreams did come true. Two months from now she would walk down those stairs in a real wedding gown.

Zack paced the floor of Sterling Kilgannon's study, well aware that the men in this room were rooting for him to survive his pre-wedding jitters even if they were laughing at him.

"What are you worried about, Zack?" Collin asked. "That your bride will jilt you for a podiatrist?"

That wouldn't have been funny to most people, but in this room of doctors, that was high humor. What *was* funny was seeing all five of them wearing the same thing—white tuxes and blue bow ties. His grand-father and Chloe's father wore the basic outfit while his two best men—his uncle Albert and Collin—Zack couldn't decide who should get top billing—also wore blue vests that matched Carmen and Chloe's dresses. As the groom, his vest was white. Cate claimed the wedding party colour scheme had come to her in a vision, and Chloe and Carmen had laughingly backed her up. Of course, he was curious but getting to the altar was more important to him than what they wore to get there.

Chloe's supervisor from Love Into Action, an ordained minister, stuck his head in the door. "Hi everybody. Can I run you through the plan again?"

Albert welcomed him in, and Zack tried to focus on what was said, but it didn't get through. All he could think of was that in thirty minutes or less, Chloe would be his bride.

The mirror in Chloe's mother's room was the biggest in the house. Dressed in her beautiful wedding gown, Chloe stood before it and realized the bride in the mirror was not only joyously happy, she was really pretty.

For Chloe to believe that about herself was amazing. Her sisters had done wonders for her confidence, and they'd taught her how to make the most of her looks, but seeing herself through Zack's eyes had made the difference.

"You look so beautiful, Chloe," Carmen said, dabbing a tear with her finger.

"No crying!" Cate ordered. "We are *not* going to ruin our makeup just because Chloe's gorgeous, *she* has a wonderful man to love her, and we don't!" Cate and Carmen let out pretend wails that sounded so genuine they made Chloe laugh.

But their mother came running. "What is it?" she shrieked. "Just don't tell me the wedding's off, not after all I've gone through this last month."

Cate slung her arm over her mother's shoulders.

"Sorry, Mom, Carmen and I were just letting off steam. We're so jealous that Chloe's the bride."

"You girls will get your turn someday."

Chloe smiled at the conversation. It was so nice, all of them together like this. All of them but Bonnie. "Has anyone seen Bonnie? She and Amy are supposed to be with us before we go downstairs."

"I'm on it," Cate said, pulling out her cell phone.

There was a rap on the door, and the wedding planner eased into the room with a big box of flowers. "Here you go, ladies. Beautiful bride, this is your bouquet. Gorgeous bridesmaids, these are for you. Ava! You're too young to be mother of the bride, but you can wear her corsage anyway."

"Bonnie and Amy are sitting with the guests!" Cate reported. "But they're on their way."

"While we're waiting," the wedding planner said, "let's talk about your entrance. We do it just like we rehearsed."

Zack waited at the bottom of the Kilgannons' grand curved staircase to greet Amy Brennan. He escorted her to the front row and went back for Mom, who was so pretty in her elegant blue dress. His heart swelled with love. She'd brought Chloe into his life, and both of them had shown him God's love.

Mom's chair was beside Amy's. He kissed them both and took his place with the minister under an arch of fragrant white flowers.

It was Sterling's turn at the bottom of the stairs, waiting to escort Ava. Bright colors were her signature, but tonight Ava wore blue for Chloe.

Carmen was next, her dark beauty even more stunning than Ava's. She seemed to float down the stairs in her blue bridesmaid gown. She'd been a great friend, and Zack prayed that she'd find someone worthy to love her. Albert met her and the two of them came to stand with Zack.

Cate practically danced down the stairs, wearing a matching blue gown and a whole lot of spunk. She would find a great guy, but he would be the one needing prayer. Collin brought her to stand with him by Zack's side.

"Are you ready, brother?" Collin whispered.

"Piece of cake, brother," Zack whispered back, though, truthfully, he was edgy from waiting.

At the top of the stairs, Chloe scanned the crowd until she saw him and smiled. It was a glorious, fabulous smile just for him, and for him, there was no one else in the room.

Her eyes on him, she walked down the stairs. He couldn't have looked away if he'd wanted to. Without thinking he put his hand on his heart. She took his breath away. He would love this beautiful woman until his dying day.

Her dad met her and offered his arm. "I love you, Chloe."

She'd waited a lifetime to hear that. Tears filled her eyes, and she looked up to see if he meant it.

He did! He brought out a lady's handkerchief with her name embroidered in blue! "Mom said you might need this."

Chloe glanced at her mother and felt such a rush of love.

"Ready to move on?" her dad asked. "Zack can't wait to be my son-in-law."

Dad walked her to Zack, her handsome groom. Her sisters straightened the hem of her gown, and she looked up at Zack.

"Everything okay?" he whispered.

"Perfect," she murmured, and it was. Her boss from work was the most loving minister she knew, and he guided the exchange of their vows with great sensitivity.

They had no poems to read to each other. They had no handwritten vows. For them, the part that mattered came after the exchange of rings when the minister pronounced them husband and wife.

He might have told them they could kiss. Chloe didn't hear that or even know when the kiss started. She just knew Zack was hers to love forever.

"C'mon, man," she heard Collin whisper. "Save something for later."

"What do you think, Chloe?" Zack murmured against her lips.

People *were* starting to chuckle. But, then, weren't they all family and friends?

"I don't think they'll mind just one…"

She didn't get to finish that thought. Zack had claimed another kiss, and their guests didn't seem to mind at all.

Kisses from her husband and a lifetime of loving him back. It was more than she had dared to dream of and more than her highest hope.

* * * * *

Dear Reader,

I hope you're not in the middle of heartache right now, but I'm sure you know what it feels like. We all do. Some time ago I read the Living Bible translation of Ephesians 3:20–21. It's a comforting passage in any translation, but this version lifted my heart at a moment when I really needed it: "Now glory be to God who…is able to do far more than we would ever dare to ask or even dream of—infinitely beyond our highest prayers, desires, thoughts, or hopes."

In this story, Chloe knows God has that kind of power, but she forgets that she should "dare to ask" or expect blessings "beyond her highest hopes." I have a problem remembering that myself.

My 2008 New Year's resolution is to dream big, ask largely, praise Him generously and surrender what I think I want so the Lord can supply what *He* wants for me.

Please visit my Web site, www.pattmarr.com. You can e-mail me from there or write to me at P.O. Box 13, Silvis, IL 61282. Hearing from you is such an encouragement. Tell me something about yourself, what you like to read or what you want me to pray about.

In Him,

Patt Marr

QUESTIONS FOR DISCUSSION

1. Zack and Chloe fall for each other quickly. Does it matter how long a couple knows each other before they marry? Why or why not?

2. Chloe loved her work with children and doesn't understand why God would take that away. She learns that He has another plan for her, a plan that provides her heart's desire. Have you lost something dear to you and later discovered it was for your good?

3. Bonnie asks Chloe what she sees herself doing in five years. It seems like a good idea to have goals, but how do Christians answer that, knowing that God has a plan for our lives—and we don't know it? What do you want in life?

4. Chloe seems to fall into the typical middle-child syndrome. (Adored eldest, spoiled youngest, forgotten middle.) Yet she doesn't hold this against her sisters Carmen and Cate. Where do you fall in the birth order of your family? How does this affect your relationship with your siblings? Your parents?

5. At the Hilltop restaurant, Chloe is nervous and her silverware falls to the floor. Zack's silverware falls, too—on purpose. Is that modern-day chivalry? Have you ever done something embarrassing to make another person feel better?

6. Zack invites Carmen to have dinner with him and Chloe in order to fend off his mother's matchmaking. Have you ever had to do something to stop a friend or relative's relentless matchmaking? What was it? How did the situation turn out?

7. The night before his mother leaves Los Angeles, Zack learns that his mother paid a high price for bad choices she made as a young woman. Can you relate to Bonnie's regret? Why or why not?

8. Chloe has no problem believing she's exceptionally intelligent, but she can't believe she's pretty. Have you known people who can believe one truth about themselves, but not another?

9. Zack and Chloe both have fathers who've embarrassed and hurt them. How did they deal with their fathers and how did it turn out? Do you think having this in common brought them closer together?

10. Because of an unforeseen illness, Chloe cannot have children. She puts off telling Zack about it until they are engaged. Do you think this was the right thing to do? If you were in her situation, what would you have done?

LOVE INSPIRED HISTORICAL
*Powerful, engaging stories of romance, adventure
and faith set in the past—when life was simpler
and faith played a major role in everyday lives.
Turn the page for a sneak preview of*
THE BRITON
by
Catherine Palmer
*Love Inspired Historical—love and faith
throughout the ages
A brand-new line from Steeple Hill Books
Launching this February!*

"Welcome to the family, Briton," said one of Olaf's men in a mocking voice. "We look forward to the presence of a woman at our hall."

Bronwen grasped her tunic and yanked it from the Viking's thick fingers. As she stepped away from the table, she heard the drunken laughter of the barbarians behind her. How could her father have betrothed her to the old Viking?

Running down the stone steps toward the heavy oak door that led outside the keep, Bronwen gathered her mantle about her. She ordered the doorman to open it, and he did so reluctantly, pressing her to carry a torch. But Bronwen pushed past him and fled into the darkness.

Dashing down the steep, pebbled hill toward the beach, she felt the frozen ground give way to sand. She threw off her veil and circlet and kicked away her shoes.

Racing alongside the pounding surf, she felt hot tears

of anger and shame well up and stream down her cheeks. With no concern for her safety, Bronwen ran and ran, her long braids streaming behind her, falling loose, drifting like a tattered black flag.

Blinded with weeping, she did not see the dark form that loomed suddenly in her path and stopped dead her headlong sprint. Bronwen shrieked in surprise and fear as iron arms pinned her and a heavy cloak threatened to suffocate her.

"Release me!" she cried. "Guard! Guard, help me!"

"Hush, my lady." A deep voice emanated from the darkness. "I mean you no harm. What demon drives you to run so madly in the night without fear for your safety?"

"Release me, villain! I am the daughter—"

"I shall hold you until you calm yourself. We had heard there were witches in Amounderness, but I had not thought to meet one so openly."

Still held tight in the man's arms, Bronwen drew back and peered up at the hooded figure. "You! You are the man who spied on our feast. Release me at once, or I shall call the guard upon you."

The man chuckled at this and turned toward his companions, who stood in a group nearby. Bronwen caught hold of the back of his hood and jerked it down to reveal a head of glossy raven curls. But the man's face was shrouded in darkness yet, and as he looked at her, she could not read his expression.

"So you are the blessed bride-to-be." He pulled the hood back over his head. "Your father has paired you with an interesting choice."

Relieved that her captor did not appear to be a highwayman, she sagged from his warm hands onto the wet sand. "Please leave me here alone. I need peace to think. Go on your way."

The tall stranger shrugged off his outer mantle and wrapped it around her shoulders. "Why did your father betroth you thus to the aged Viking?" he asked.

"For one purported to be a spy, you know precious little about Amounderness. But I shall tell you, as it is all common knowledge."

She pulled the cloak tightly about her, reveling in its warmth. "Our land, Amounderness, once was Briton territory. Olaf Lothbrok, my betrothed, came here as a youth when the Viking invasions had nearly subsided. He took the lands directly to the south of Rossall Hall from their Briton lord. Then, of course, the Normans came, and Amounderness was pillaged by William the Conqueror's army."

The man squatted on the sand beside Bronwen. He listened with obvious interest as she continued the familiar tale. "When William took an account of Amounderness in his Domesday Book, he recorded no remaining lords and few people at all. But he did not know the Britons. Slowly, we crept out of hiding and returned to our halls. My father's family reoccupied Rossall Hall. And there we live, as we should, watching over our serfs as they fish and grow their meager crops. Indeed, there is not much here for the greedy Normans to want, if they are the ones for whom you spy."

Unwilling to continue speaking when her heart was so heavy, Bronwen stood and turned toward the sea. The traveler rose beside her and touched her arm. "Olaf Lothbrok's lands—together with your father's—will reunite most of Amounderness. A clever plan. Your sister's future husband holds the rest of the adjoining lands, I understand."

"You've done your work, sir. Your lord will be pleased. Who is he—some land-hungry Scottish baron? Or have you forgotten that King Stephen gave Amounderness to the Scots as a trade for the support in his war with Matilda? I certainly hope your lord is not a Norman. He would be so disappointed to learn he has no legal rights here. Now, if you will excuse me?"

Bronwen turned and began walking back along the beach toward Rossall Hall. She felt better for her run, and somehow her father's plan did not seem so far-fetched anymore. Distant lights twinkled through the fog that was rolling in from the west, and she suddenly realized what a long way she had come.

"My lady," the stranger's voice called out behind her.

Bronwen kept walking, unwilling to face again the one who had seen her in her humiliation. She did not care what he reported to his master.

"My lady, you have a bit of a walk ahead of you." The traveler strode forward to join her. "Perhaps I should accompany you to your destination."

"You leave me no choice, I see."

"I am not one to compromise myself, dear lady. I follow the path God has set before me and none other."

"And just who are you?"

"I am called Jacques."

"French. A Norman, as I had suspected."

The man chuckled. "Not nearly as Norman as you are Briton."

As they approached the fortress, Bronwen could see that the guests had not yet begun to disperse. Perhaps no one had missed her and she could slip quietly into bed beside Gildan.

She turned to go, but he took her arm and studied her face in the moonlight. Then, gently, he drew her into the folds of his hooded cloak. "Perhaps the bride would like the memory of a younger man's embrace to warm her," he whispered.

Astonished, Bronwen attempted to remove his arms from around her waist. But she could not escape his lips as they found her own. The kiss was soft and warm, melting away her resistance like the sun upon the snow. Before she had time to react, he was striding back down the beach.

Bronwen stood stunned for a moment, clutching his woolen mantle about her. Suddenly she cried out, "Wait, Jacques! Your mantle!"

The dark one turned to her. "Keep it for now," he shouted into the wind. "I shall ask for it when we meet again."

* * * * *

Don't miss this deeply moving
Love Inspired Historical story about
a medieval lady who finds strength in
God to save her family legacy—and
to open her heart to love.

THE BRITON
by Catherine Palmer
available February 2008

And also look for
HOMESPUN BRIDE
by Jillian Hart,
where a Montana woman discovers
that love is the greatest blessing of all.

REQUEST YOUR FREE BOOKS!

2 FREE INSPIRATIONAL NOVELS
PLUS 2
FREE
MYSTERY GIFTS

Love Inspired

YES! Please send me 2 FREE Love Inspired® novels and my 2 FREE mystery gifts. After receiving them, if I don't wish to receive any more books, I can return the shipping statement marked "cancel." If I don't cancel, I will receive 4 brand-new novels every month and be billed just $3.99 per book in the U.S., or $4.74 per book in Canada, plus 25¢ shipping and handling per book and applicable taxes, if any*. That's a savings of 20% off the cover price! I understand that accepting the 2 free books and gifts places me under no obligation to buy anything. I can always return a shipment and cancel at any time. Even if I never buy another book from Steeple Hill, the two free books and gifts are mine to keep forever.

113 IDN EF26   313 IDN EF27

Name _____ (PLEASE PRINT)

Address _____ Apt. #

City _____ State/Prov. _____ Zip/Postal Code

Signature (if under 18, a parent or guardian must sign)

Order online at www.LoveInspiredBooks.com

Or mail to Steeple Hill Reader Service™:

IN U.S.A.: P.O. Box 1867, Buffalo, NY 14240-1867
IN CANADA: P.O. Box 609, Fort Erie, Ontario L2A 5X3

Not valid to current Love Inspired subscribers.

Want to try two free books from another series?
Call 1-800-873-8635 or visit www.morefreebooks.com

* Terms and prices subject to change without notice. NY residents add applicable sales tax. Canadian residents will be charged applicable provincial taxes and GST. This offer is limited to one order per household. All orders subject to approval. Credit or debit balances in a customer's account(s) may be offset by any other outstanding balance owed by or to the customer. Please allow 4 to 6 weeks for delivery.

Your Privacy: Steeple Hill is committed to protecting your privacy. Our Privacy Policy is available online at www.eHarlequin.com or upon request from the Reader Service. From time to time we make our lists of customers available to reputable firms who may have a product or service of interest to you. If you would prefer we not share your name and address, please check here. ☐

LIREG07

INTRODUCING

Love Inspired.
HISTORICAL

A NEW TWO-BOOK SERIES.

Every month, acclaimed
inspirational authors
will bring you engaging stories
rich with romance, adventure
and faith set in a variety
of vivid historical times.

History begins on **February 12**
wherever you buy books.

Steeple
Hill®

www.SteepleHill.com

Love Inspired®

When four little noisemakers moved in next door to Wade Dalton, he didn't expect he'd fall for the kids and their beautiful aunt. With Cassie being at least a dozen years his junior and Wade having a secret that would only make life harder for them, he had to keep his distance, but that was something those four little blessings weren't about to let him do!

Look for

Four Little Blessings

by

Merrillee Whren

Available February
wherever books are sold.

Love Inspired

TITLES AVAILABLE NEXT MONTH

Don't miss these four stories in February

A DREAM TO SHARE by Irene Hannon
Heartland Homecoming

Mark Campbell was in Missouri to convince Abby Warner to sell her family's newspaper to his conglomerate. He didn't want to spend any more time in the one-stoplight town than he had to. But the feisty newswoman brought out feelings in Mark that were front-page worthy.

HEALING TIDES by Lois Richer
Pennies from Heaven

Doctors aren't supposed to get attached to patients, yet GloryAnn Cranbrook couldn't help falling for one sick little boy. He needed a procedure only her boss, Dr. Jared Steele, could perform. So why wouldn't he do it? It was up to GloryAnn to change his mind—and his heart.

FOUR LITTLE BLESSINGS by Merrillee Whren

The four little noisemakers who'd moved next door to Wade Dalton came with a bonus: their beautiful aunt. Wade was attracted to the chaos that surrounded them, though he had a secret that could keep them all apart. Something the four little blessings weren't about to let happen.

HER UNLIKELY FAMILY by Missy Tippens

Her calling was to help teenage runaways. But when the handsome, uptight uncle of her newest girl showed up, Josie Miller knew she was in over her head. Michael Throckmorton didn't know the first thing about parenting. Maybe she could help them all become a family.

LICNM0108